THE GEORGIA REGIONAL
LIBRARY FOR THE BLIND
AND PHYSICALLY
HANDICAPPED IS A FREE
SERVICE FOR INDIVIDUALS
UNABLE TO READ
STANDARD PRINT.

ASK AT OUR CIRCULATION
DESK HOW TO REGISTER
FOR THIS SERVICE, AS WELL
AS OTHER SERVICES
OFFERED BY THIS LIBRARY.

THE COLOR OF COURAGE

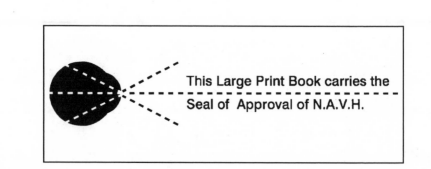

This Large Print Book carries the
Seal of Approval of N.A.V.H.

THE COLOR OF COURAGE

PATRICIA DAVIDS

THORNDIKE PRESS
A part of Gale, Cengage Learning

GALE
CENGAGE Learning™

Detroit • New York • San Francisco • New Haven, Conn • Waterville, Maine • London

GALE
CENGAGE Learning™

LIBRARY OF CONGRESS CATALOGING-IN-PUBLICATION DATA

Davids, Patricia.
　The color of courage / by Patricia Davids.
　　p. cm. — (Thorndike Press large print Christian fiction)
　ISBN-13: 978-1-4104-0486-2 (hardcover : alk. paper)
　ISBN-10: 1-4104-0486-2 (hardcover : alk. paper)
　1. Women soldiers — Fiction. 2. Brothers — Death — Fiction.
　3. Horses — Wounds and injuries — Fiction. 4. Veterinarians —
　Fiction. 5. Large type books. I. Title.
　PS3604.A9454C66 2008
　813'.6—dc22　　　　　　　　　　　　　　　　　　　2007044712

Published in 2008 by arrangement with Harlequin Books S.A.

Printed in the United States of America
1 2 3 4 5 6 7 12 11 10 09 08

A man's heart plans his way,
But the Lord directs his steps.
— Proverbs 16:9

To Joshua. You're the best grandson in
the world, honey.
Now get those grades up!

And to all the men and women serving
in the United States military. Please
accept my thanks
and my humble gratitude.

PROLOGUE

"Lindsey . . . I need you . . . to do this."

Standing beside her brother's hospital bed, Sergeant Lindsey Mandel fought back tears. She held his hand though she knew he couldn't feel it. "Danny, what if it doesn't work out?"

"You'll make it work . . . I know you will." He spoke quickly because he could only talk when the ventilator keeping him alive breathed out.

She brushed her hand over his close-shaven head. He was six years older than she was, thirty-one to her twenty-five. Today, he looked decades older than when she had seen him three months ago. "Don't give up, Danny. You can still get better."

A wry smile twisted his lips. "Who are you . . . kidding?" What might have been a chuckle turned into a cough and an alarm sounded from the monitor above his bed.

Frightened, Lindsey glanced to Danny's

wife, Abigail, sitting on the other side of the bed. Behind her, the door to the room opened and a nurse in green scrubs looked in. The beeping stopped and Abigail waved the woman away. "It's all right. He just needs to stop talking for a while."

Admiring her sister-in-law's calm, Lindsey willed herself to relax. Abigail rose, moved to Lindsey's side and asked, "Why don't we go grab a cup of coffee?"

"Good idea. . . . Get her . . . out of here . . . for a while."

Abigail leaned down and kissed his forehead. "You just want us to leave so you can flirt with the cute nurses."

"Rats . . . you found . . . me out." He closed his eyes.

Lindsey leaned down to kiss him, too. "I'll be back," she promised.

He nodded, but his eyes remained closed. He looked so weary. When she turned to go, she heard him say, "I'm proud of you . . . First Sergeant . . . Mandel."

A heavy band of emotion squeezed her heart. "I'm proud of you, too, Master Sergeant Mandel."

"Don't spend . . . your whole leave . . . in this hospital."

"I'll spend my leave anywhere I choose," she retorted.

A fleeting smile crossed his face. "Head-strong . . . as ever."

"Because you raised me that way. Stop talking and rest."

Outside of his room, Lindsey paused as several men in uniform walked past, pushing others in wheelchairs. Everywhere she looked, the halls of Walter Reed hospital bustled with activity. Walking silently beside Abigail to a small waiting room, Lindsey waited until her sister-in-law filled two cups from the vending machine. Dressed in a pair of rumpled beige slacks and a wrinkled mauve shirt with her dark hair pulled back haphazardly into a silver clip, Abigail looked worn to the bone.

"The coffee isn't good, but I've had worse." She handed one to Lindsey.

Lindsey stirred a packet of creamer into the piping brew. "I can't believe Danny wants me to take Dakota away. He loves that horse. He's given up, hasn't he?"

Initially, her brother's will to live in spite of his injuries had helped Lindsey cope, but the unfairness of it all weighed on her.

Abigail gestured toward the red vinyl chairs lining the wall. "Why don't we sit down. I don't think he has given up. He's just coming to terms with the reality of the situation. The shrapnel severed his spine.

11

He's a quadriplegic. After three months of therapy, he knows he isn't going to get much better."

"But there's still hope."

"The doctors think, with work, he'll be able to breathe on his own, but he'll never ride again. Yes, he loves that horse. That's why he wants you to take Dakota back to Fort Riley with you."

"Danny has lost so much already. It doesn't seem right to take Dakota away, too."

"Look around you, Lindsey. Most of the men and women who are patients here were wounded in action. Do you know what the majority of them say they want? To stay in the service. To get back to their units. Danny knows he can never go back, but he needs to do something positive. He feels he can do that by donating Dakota to your unit. You have no idea how excited he was when he heard about your transfer into the mounted color guard last year."

"Danny tried to transfer into the Third Infantry a number of times. The Old Guard has a mounted unit. Why not donate Dakota to them? That way Dakota would still be in Washington, D.C., and Danny could go and see him when he's better."

"I thought about that, but the Old Guard

12

only takes black, gray or white horses. Your unit takes bays."

Brown horses with black manes and tails and minimal white markings were the traditional mounts of the Seventh Cavalry, the regiment Lindsey's unit portrayed at Fort Riley, Kansas. Dakota wouldn't be excluded for that reason, but less than half of the horses brought to the fort passed the intensive training requirements.

"What if he isn't suitable for us? Then what?"

"He's just got to be, Lindsey. Please, make this work. It would mean so much to Danny. He desperately needs something to look forward to, or else — or else I'm afraid to think about what could happen."

CHAPTER ONE

Leaning forward in the saddle, Lindsey patted Dakota's neck and tried to quell her
nervousness. "This is it, boy. This is your
final test. You have to get this right."

The dark brown gelding responded by
tossing his head and pulling at the reins as
if to show her that he was eager to get down
to business. She couldn't help but smile.

Running a hand down her mount's sleek,
muscular neck, she found the calmness she
needed. She drew a deep, cleansing breath.
The cool breeze carried the smell of dust,
fallen leaves and the earthy scent of horses.
Looking over the fence to the hills rising
just beyond the road, she saw the golden-
hued stone buildings of old Fort Riley
where they stood nestled between oaks,
elms and sycamores bearing the first touches
of fall colors. Dakota pulled impatiently at
the reins again.

"Okay, I'm the one stalling," she admitted. "I just want this so badly — for you and me, but mostly for Danny."

Each week her brother called for updates about Dakota's training, offering advice and pointers that she didn't really need but accepted anyway. Today, he would be waiting impatiently for her call. She intended to give him good news.

Reaching down, she checked that her saber and rifle would slide easily out of their scabbard and boot. The reproduction models of the 1860s U.S. Cavalry equipment were spotless after her careful preparations that morning. Even the brass buttons of her blue wool cavalry jacket gleamed brightly in the late-morning sun. She was as ready as she could get.

Be with us today, Lord, for Danny's sake.

At the touch of her heels, Dakota bounded forward. Together, they sailed over a series of low jumps, then slid to a halt and whirled back at the end of the field. On the return run, Lindsey drew her saber and headed into a series of poles topped with red and white balloons. As Dakota wove in and out, she slashed left and right, breaking as many as she could. He didn't even flinch at the loud pops or the swish of the sword cutting close beside him.

Four men on horseback waited for her at

the end of the course. She slowed to a trot. Each man drew his saber and held it over his head with the tip pointing backward. One by one she struck their swords with her own as she passed close behind them, making the steel weapons ring with bell-like tones.

Sheathing her saber, she drew her pistols. Digging her heels into her mount's sides, she headed into the jumps again, this time blasting the balloons with her revolvers. Dakota raced on without faltering until they cleared the last hurdle. Only one maneuver remained.

Holstering her guns, she pulled the horse to a sliding stop and dismounted. Drawing her carbine rifle from its boot, she gave a low command, lifted Dakota's foreleg and pulled his head around. "Throwing the Horse" was the hardest movement for the young gelding to perform. Many horses refused the command.

To her relief, Dakota knelt, then lay down and rolled onto his side without hesitation.

"Stay down," she ordered. Stretching out behind his back, Lindsey rested her rifle on his shoulder and fired off three rounds. They were only blanks, but the sharp reports were as loud as if they had been real bullets. Dakota jerked slightly at the sound of the first discharge, but remained quietly on his side, providing lifesaving cover for his rider as cavalry horses have been trained to do through the ages.

As the echoes of the last shot died away, Lindsey rose to her feet and gave the command to stand. After scrambling to his feet, Dakota shook himself and waited patiently for her to remount. She wanted to throw her arms around his neck and hug him, but not now, not yet.

"Good boy, you were perfect. Just perfect," she murmured as she swung up into the saddle. She knew she was grinning like a fool, but she couldn't help it. After only three months of training, Dakota had proved himself worthy of a place in the elite Commanding General's Mounted Color Guard at Fort Riley. Danny would be so proud.

She returned to the end of the field, where other members of her unit sat on their horses. Beside the men, Captain Jeffery Watson, her unit commander, stood with his arms crossed and a faint frown on his face. Stopping in front of him, Lindsey saluted smartly.

"Well done, Sergeant Mandel."

"Thank you, sir."

The other men in her unit gathered around. "You looked fine out there." Private

18

Avery Barnes was the next to offer his opinion. The dark-haired Boston native pushed his cap back to smile at her with a roguish grin.

"She always looks good. It was Dakota who looked great," drawled Corporal Shane Ross as he leaned over and patted the horse's neck. It was no secret the tall blond Texan was fond of all the four-legged members of the unit. He took as much pride in their skill as he did in the abilities of the horses' human partners.

"So, does this mean Dakota is in?" the third soldier queried. Private Lee Gillis, the newest enlisted member of the mounted color guard was watching their captain closely.

Captain Watson reached out to rub Dakota's cheek. "I will admit that I was worried when I learned that Dakota belonged to your brother, Sergeant."

Lindsey gave him a puzzled look. "May I ask why?"

"The last thing I wanted to do was to tell a wounded veteran that his horse wasn't suitable for our unit. Thanks to your hard work, I won't have to do that. I think Dakota makes a fine addition to our stable."

She nearly melted with relief as the men around her grinned and offered their congratulations. "Thank you, sir. I know I speak for my brother when I say that it is an honor to have Dakota accepted."

Crossing his arms again, the captain allowed a smile to soften his stern features. "As the icing on this cake, I wanted you all to know that I just received word from the Joint Task Force-Armed Forces Inaugural Committee that the Commanding General's Mounted Color Guard had been invited to participate in the upcoming Presidential Inauguration parade."

A cheer of excitement went up from the men. Lindsey grinned at their enthusiasm, "That's wonderful news, sir. Will Dakota be going, too?"

"Dakota has earned his place. And, of course, as the highest ranking non-commissioned officer, you will be the U.S. flag bearer for our unit. I'm sure you'll want to ride Dakota for that, but if you prefer another mount, I'll understand."

"Oh, no, I'll be riding Dakota." Wait until she told Danny. He would burst his buttons with pride.

"I've decided to include Dakota in Saturday's performance. Can he handle the crowd at a Kansas State football game?"

"I know he can, sir."

"Good. That will be all, Sergeant. Dismiss

20

the detail." Captain Watson stepped back from the horses.

Lindsey saluted, dismissed the men and then let the overwhelming happiness sink in. Being asked to participate in the Inaugural parade was an incredible honor. She might be the one bearing the flag, but she would be carrying it for her brother. Giddy with delight, she headed for the stables. This was one phone call she couldn't wait to make.

Early Saturday afternoon, Brian Cutter walked along the edge of the Kansas State University football field in Manhattan, Kansas, leaning heavily on his cane. Halftime activities for the first home game of the year were well underway. The energetic shouts of cheerleaders dressed in purple and white, the noise from thousands of fans and the blare of the band was almost deafening. But Brian had his eye on a group of halftime performers who seemed unfazed by the clamor.

Beneath the goalposts at the north end of the field, six horses stood quietly waiting for their riders. The matching bays all sported dark blue blankets and McClellan Cavalry saddles.

He had watched them being unloaded

behind the stadium and something in the third horse's gait had caught his attention. The gelding's walk wasn't quite right. Maybe it was nothing more than a bruise from the trailer ride, but he wanted to make sure the horse's rider was aware of what he'd seen. Until the horse was examined, it shouldn't be ridden.

The riders were out now and preparing to mount. Brian tried to hurry, but his bad leg was aching again. He didn't need a weatherman to tell him a cold front was moving in. Sharp pain shot through his hip and forced him to rely more heavily on his cane, making him feel much older than his thirty-two years. He arrived at the temporary picket line just as a young woman dressed in Civil War military garb was checking her saddle and girth.

"Excuse me, miss. I need a word with you." Brian knew he sounded curt and short of breath. She turned her attention on him and whatever he had intended to say flew out of his mind the way a yearling bolts out the barn door and into a summertime pasture.

She was a stunning woman. Even dressed in men's clothing did little to hide her feminine figure. The round, flat-topped soldier's cap with its short bill sat atop a mass of thick, auburn curls, but it was her eyes that captured his attention. An unusual color of silver green, they reminded him of the springtime quaking aspen near his Montana childhood home. A sprinkling of freckles dusted her cheeks and nose. Her lips were full and parted in a sweet smile.

"Yes?" she prompted. Something in her wide smile reminded him of Emily.

He pushed the ridiculous idea aside. His deceased wife and this woman didn't look alike at all.

The female soldier glanced to where the other members of the group were forming up. "You said you needed a word with me? I'm about to go on. Can you make it quick?" Her tone was polite but dismissive. He found himself irritated with her attitude.

"Your horse is lame. You shouldn't be riding him until someone looks at his right front leg."

She frowned, as if deciding whether or not to take him seriously. "Dakota seems fine to me."

To her credit, she walked around the animal and ran her hand down the horse's leg, then led him a few steps to observe him before giving Brian a frosty smile. "I don't see a problem."

"I saw it when he got off the trailer."

She swung up into the saddle with ease. Looking down at him, she managed a smile that wasn't quite polite. "We just finished a fifteen-minute warm-up. He's fine, honest. I'm sorry, but my men are waiting on me."

"You're doing the animal a disservice. You should pull him out of this exhibition until he can be examined."

"Thank you for your concern, but I know this horse better than anyone. If he were having trouble, I'd be the first to notice."

He stepped forward and laid a hand on the horse's bridle. "I'm a vet. I get paid to notice when an animal isn't moving right."

From the corner of her eye, Lindsey saw that several of the support men from her unit who weren't riding had begun to move toward her. If this guy didn't back off, he might find himself in a lot of trouble. A scene was the last thing she wanted. A big part of the CGMCG's mission was public relations.

"That may be true, but you aren't our vet. Thank you for your concern. Excuse me, I have to go."

"Suit yourself, but you'll only make him more lame. When he's limping tomorrow, remember that I told you so." He stepped aside to let her ride out and join her group.

Lindsey cast a look back at the rude man

who seemed to think he had some say in what she did. He was a little above medium height and slender, but not skinny. His gray eyes were piercing and a perfect match to the leaden sky overhead. Nicely dressed in a gray tweed sport coat over a blue button-down oxford shirt and gray slacks, he wasn't a bad-looking guy. She might even have said he was kind of cute except for his personality. *Arrogant* wasn't a strong enough word to describe him.

Dismissing the man's brusque words, Lindsey forced herself to concentrate as the unit lined up for their first maneuver. Today they would begin the exhibition by riding two by two and taking four low hurdles as a column while their bugler blew "To the Gallop." It was a sure crowd-pleaser.

Lindsey patted Dakota's neck while they waited. They were the first horse and rider in a line of three. During his warm-up, he hadn't seemed as eager as usual, but they had been training hard the past few days and they were both tired. Still, he certainly hadn't been favoring either front leg.

"We'll take a few days' rest after today, fella. How does that sound?"

Actually, it sounded like a really good idea. She hadn't realized how tired she was until her conversation with the grumpy guy.

She glanced back once more. He was watching her from the picket line. The wind blew his shaggy blond hair this way and that. The frown on his face made him look intimidating. He was rubbing his right thigh until he saw her looking. He stopped and straightened. Still scowling, he walked down the sidelines in front of the stands. She couldn't help wondering why he needed the cane. Was it a recent injury?

Perhaps the last woman he had tried to bully had kicked him in the shin. The image made Lindsey smile until she realized how unkind it was. The man had only been trying to help.

Beside them, the bugle sounded and Lindsey leaned forward as they began at a walk, then advanced to a trot and then into a gallop down the football field. Making a turn in tight formation, the horses thundered toward a row of jumps set up on the fifty yard line. As they approached the first obstacle, she felt Dakota hesitate then jump off stride. With another horse close behind them, there was no room for error.

Something was wrong. Before she could pull out of line they were on the second jump. Dakota launched forward, and she relaxed. This jump was good. He was fine.

Only he wasn't. His knees buckled when

his front feet hit the ground. He fell, cata-
pulting her forward. Lindsey threw out her
arms and tried to kick free of the stirrups.
She had an instant to breathe a prayer for
help before she felt the impact of her body
hitting the ground, followed by Dakota's
weight rolling over her.

CHAPTER TWO

Brian watched in horror as the woman and her horse went down directly in front of him. The next rider was so close behind that he couldn't turn aside and his horse fell on top of the downed pair. In a split second the precision-riding exhibition had turned into a melee.

Brian hurried toward the pileup even as the other members of the team leaped from their horses to race toward their fallen comrades. One horse scrambled to his feet and limped a few feet away. His rider sat on the ground looking dazed, with blood oozing from a cut on his forehead. The first horse that had gone down was struggling to rise but couldn't gain his feet because the rails and the pillar of the jump were tangled with his legs.

Brian didn't see the woman until he reached the horse's head, but he heard her bloodcurdling scream. She was lying face-down with her right arm pinned beneath her mount. He grabbed the horse's bridle and spoke softly. "Easy boy. Miss, lie still."

She dug the fingers of her free hand into the thick turf. "Get . . . him . . . off!"

Each word sounded as if it was being torn from her throat by unbearable pain.

Brian sank to one knee, his stiff leg stretched awkwardly out in front of him and pulled the frightened horse's head into his lap. He knew the animal's struggles could inflict more injury on the trapped rider. He stroked the gelding's cheek until he quieted. "I can't move him, yet. Help is coming."

"Is he hurt?" Her voice was muffled, but her concern was unmistakable.

"I can't tell."

She raised her head to look at him. Her hat had come off. Bright auburn curls framed her oval face in stark contrast to her frightening pallor. One cheek was smeared with dirt and scratches. When she met his gaze, her eyes gleamed with anguish and unshed tears.

"Why . . . isn't he . . . getting up?" She moaned, then bit her lip.

"His legs are caught in the jump pillar. Don't try to move. We'll get you both free in a minute."

Brian saw with relief that medical personnel were swarming onto the field. A soldier from her unit dropped to his knees beside her. "Lie still, Lindsey. How badly are you hurt?"

Lindsey dropped her head back onto the turf and sucked in a series of quick breaths. The scent of trampled grass and loamy dirt filled her nostrils. Dakota's weight was crushing her arm. Trying not to scream, she gritted her teeth and dug her fingers into the thick grass again. Screaming would only frighten the horse and make him struggle.

"I think my arm is broken."

"We'll get you free in a minute."

Please, God, let them hurry.

She felt Shane take her hand and she gripped it tightly. Don't scream, she thought, be brave. Act like a soldier. She squeezed her eyes shut and tried to stay calm. Only it was so hard. It hurt so much.

Through clenched teeth, she managed to say, "We tripped Avery . . . and Socks. Are they okay?"

Shane said, "Socks is up. Avery looks a little shaken, but I think he's okay. Hold on, kid."

"Dakota is all right, isn't he, Shane?" She panted, trying to block out the merciless agony. "Please, tell me he's all right."

"I'll check him over once we get you free." She recognized the voice as the grouchy vet who had suggested Dakota wasn't sound. If only she had heeded him instead of resenting his interference.

Pride goeth before a fall. Dear, Lord, why did I have to find that out the hard way?

She raised her head once more to look at him. "This is my fault. I should have listened to you."

Two men in EMS uniforms reached her, saving Brian from having to reply. For that, he was thankful. As they attended to Lindsey, soldiers from the unit quickly dismantled the jump and pillar, making room to move the stricken horse. With their help, Brian coaxed Dakota to roll off his side and onto his stomach, but kept the horse from rising. The move freed Lindsey's arm, but tore a scream from her that ripped into his heart.

While the medics worked on her, she kept asking about her horse. Others offered her reassurances, but Brian remained silent and avoided her pleading eyes. When she was finally placed on a stretcher and taken off the field, he breathed a sigh of relief. She obviously cared a great deal for the animal. The last thing he wanted was to have her

31

see the brave fellow put down.

For the horse was being brave. Brian's admiration of the bay gelding grew as the big fellow remained still in spite of the activity going on around him. Even though his eyes were wide, with the whites showing all around indicating pain and fear, he didn't struggle or thrash the way most horses would have.

When the area had been cleared, Brian gave up his position to a color guard member and rose awkwardly to his feet. He leaned heavily on his cane until he was sure he could take a step without falling on his face. He then moved to check out the horse's leg. There was already serious swelling below the delicate ankle joint. It didn't look good.

Several of the football officials in black-and-white striped shirts approached the group. One of them asked, "How soon can you get him off the field? We have a game to play."

"Your game will have to wait." Brian didn't bother to hide his ire.

The man Lindsey had called Shane remained crouched beside Dakota, keeping him still with a hand on the horse's neck. He ignored the officials completely. "Should we let him try to get up?"

32

Brian shook his head. "Not with the way that leg is swelling. We don't want him to do more damage. Let me get a splint on it first. My truck is parked outside the gate next to your trailers. It's white with College of Veterinary Medicine in purple lettering on the side. I've got first-aid equipment in there."

"Private Gillis will get what you need if you'll give him your keys."

One of the soldiers stepped forward and held out his hand. After giving him a detailed list of what he wanted and where it was located, Brian waited impatiently for the Private's return. It seemed to take forever, but in reality only a few minutes had passed when the breathless soldier raced back and handed Brian his kit and the supplies he had requested.

With the help of the other color guard members, Brian soon had the leg encased in a cotton wool wrap. He applied a lightweight but sturdy aluminum splint and secured it with Velcro straps.

"All right, let him try and get up, but if he doesn't make it on the first attempt, we'll need to get a lift in here."

"We'll get one, but I sure hope we don't need it. Do you think he has a fracture?"

"I do, but I can't say for sure until we get

him to the clinic and X-ray the leg."

With a gentle tug on the reins and some quiet words of encouragement, Shane urged Dakota to stand. After a brief hesitation, the horse lurched awkwardly to his feet. The crowd in the stands broke into loud cheering and applause. Brian looked up in surprise. He had forgotten he had several thousand onlookers watching his every move. No doubt some of his students were in attendance. Perhaps he'd present a pop quiz on splint application on Monday to check if they had been paying attention.

"If you can get your trailer in here, I think he can be loaded. The ride to the clinic isn't far. You'll need to wedge him in securely. I don't want him moving around at all."

"Thanks, Doc. It is *doctor,* isn't it? I'm Corporal Shane Ross." He held out his hand.

Brian took it in a firm grip. "Yes, I'm Dr. Brian Cutter, Professor of Equine Surgery for the College of Veterinary Medicine here at K-State."

"Then it sounds like Dakota will be in good hands. I sure hope this isn't a serious injury. The horse belonged to Lindsey's brother. She'll never forgive herself if he has to be put down."

Lindsey endured her examination at the base hospital in stoic silence, answering between clenched lips only the questions posed to her. The pain she could deal with, but the fact that her arm hung useless against her side had her truly frightened. She couldn't even move her fingers — they had no feeling at all. Thoughts of Danny's paralysis crowded in her head. She fought down her rising panic as she addressed the physician attending her. "Sir, why can't I move my hand?"

The gray-haired doctor sat on a stool beside her narrow bed. "Your humerus is fractured, that's the bone in your upper arm. I'm going to splint it for now and send you to see an orthopedist. This is a nasty break."

Like she needed anyone to tell her that. "I still don't understand why I can't move my fingers."

"The nerve that controls hand movement runs in a grove along the bone of the upper arm. When a break occurs the nerve is often damaged. You should recover full use of your hand in a few months."

"Months?" She couldn't believe what she

was hearing.

"You'll be on restricted duty until then. I'm giving you some pain medication. Take it regularly, don't try to tough it out. I'll write some instructions on icing the arm and have the nurse make an appointment with the specialist. Do you have any questions?"

"How soon can I ride?"

"Not for at least eight weeks, maybe longer depending on the nerve damage."

She turned her face away, not wanting him to see the distress she knew was written there. The Inauguration was only ten weeks away. Did this mean there wouldn't be a trip to Washington, D.C., for her?

No, she wouldn't accept that. She wouldn't let her chance to honor Danny and all he had stood for pass by without a fight. Besides, even if she couldn't ride, Dakota could make the trip. Danny could still watch him striding down Pennsylvania Avenue. Every recent phone conversation with her sister-in-law had been filled with stories of Danny's determination to attend the parade in person.

"You won't be able to drive," the doctor said gently. "Do you have someone who can get you home?"

She nodded. Captain Watson was waiting

for her. Exactly how she was going to get back and forth from her off-base apartment to her duty station until she *could* drive was a worry she'd put aside until later.

After they applied the splint and sling and gave her some pain medication, she managed to walk out of the room under her own somewhat shaky power. She found Captain Watson perched on the edge of a chair in the waiting area. He looked nervous and ill at ease. Her heart sank.

Bracing herself to hear the worst, she asked, "How's Dakota?"

Captain Watson sprang to his feet at the sound of her voice. "I haven't heard. How are you?"

She gave a rueful glance at her big blue sling. "My arm is broken. The doctor said I'll be on restricted duty for at least eight weeks, but it may be longer than that before I regain the use of my hand."

"If you're released, I'll drive you home."

"I need to find out how Dakota is."

"Shane and Lee are with him. As soon as they know something, they'll call. You are going straight home and that's an order."

"With all due respect, sir, I need to be with him. Please?" For a moment, she thought he was going to refuse, then his shoulders slumped in defeat.

"All right. They took him to the veterinary clinic at K-State. I'll take you, but only because I want to see how he is doing myself."

"Thanks. I just need to get these prescriptions filled and then I'm ready."

Half an hour later, they pulled up to the large, white stone buildings on the outskirts of the college campus that comprised the veterinary teaching hospital. Signs at the entrance to the driveway directed them to the Large Animal Clinic at the back of the building. Lindsey's pain pills were making her woozy, but she tried to hide it. She suspected that the Captain would drive her straight home if she showed any sign of weakness. Inside the building, they found the waiting area. The long, narrow room had panels of fluorescent lights across the ceiling that seemed to glare back painfully into her eyes from the shiny, beige linoleum floor.

The far end of the room was taken up by a wide reception desk where a pretty, young blond woman was talking on the phone. An American flag stood proudly displayed near the front of the desk. Lee and Shane were seated on the one of several mauve utilitarian chairs with bare wooden arms that lined the walls. They both rose and saluted when they caught sight of their captain. They were all still dressed in their exhibition uniforms and they were gathering odd looks from the staff and clients waiting with them.

Captain Watson returned the salute. "Any word yet?"

"No, sir. The doc hasn't been out to talk to us."

"That doesn't sound good." Lindsey settled gingerly on the couch but still took a quick, indrawn hiss as pain shot through her arm and shoulder. For a second, the room spun wildly and she grabbed hold of Shane's arm.

"Easy, kid. Are you sure you're okay?"

"The pain medicine they gave me is making me light-headed, that's all."

When the room stopped spinning, she looked up to see the vet from the stadium crossing the room toward them. His thick blond hair was still mussed, but he had traded his sport jacket for a white lab coat.

He stopped in front of the group, but his gaze rested on her. Frowning, he said, "I'm surprised to see you here. How's your arm?"

The unrelenting, throbbing pain was almost unbearable. "It's broken," she snapped. "I want to hear about my horse."

Shane laid a hand on her good shoulder. "Lindsey, this is Dr. Brian Cutter. He's been looking after Dakota. Doctor, this is Sergeant Lindsey Mandel. I don't think you two managed introductions with all that happened earlier."

Lindsey realized that she must have sounded rude. The fiery agony in her arm wasn't helping her disposition. She rose to her feet and was pleased when she stayed upright. "I'm sorry, Doctor. I'm just really worried about Dakota. How is he?"

"He has a fracture of the plantar proximal eminences of the second phalanx."

Lee glanced around the group, then said, "Do you want to try that again in English for those of us who are new to all this horsey stuff?"

Dr. Cutter looked confused by Lee's statement. "I assumed you are all expert horsemen."

Captain Watson smiled in amusement. "My soldiers come from the ranks of ordinary units assigned to Fort Riley either as volunteers or as transfers. No previous riding skill is required. The men receive instruction from manuals used by Civil War cavalrymen. Private Gillis has only been with us a few weeks."

Lee grinned. "I'd never ridden a horse before then, so I still have a lot to learn."

Dr. Cutter managed a thin smile. "I see.

All right, the animal has a fracture in one of the bones in the pastern joint between his ankle and his hoof."

If Lindsey hadn't been so upset herself, the look of horror on Lee's face might have been comical when he said, "They shoot horses for that, don't they?"

Dr. Cutter frowned sharply. "We are long past the days of shooting horses here. If an animal does have to be euthanized, we use humane methods."

Lindsey sank onto the chair's edge before her legs gave out and tried to gather her scattered thoughts. "What can be done for him?"

"You have several options but the best one is surgical arthrodesis. That means we fuse the joint using special pins and a bone graft from his hip. His recovery should take about four months."

Lindsey bit her lower lip. Dakota wasn't going to Washington, D.C. It was so unfair. Why had God given her a chance to do something special for her brother only to snatch it away?

Dr. Cutter raked a hand through his hair, giving Lindsey a clue as to why it looked unkempt. "Actually, I am hoping to begin trials of a new procedure using an experimental gene therapy that will speed healing,

41

and this type of fracture is exactly the type I'm looking to study. Unfortunately, I haven't received grant approval yet."

The captain asked, "Will Dakota be able to return to duty?"

"A horse can lead a normal life after a fusion. Some horses have even returned to being successful athletes. There are, of course, risks involved, as with any surgery."

Lindsey studied his face, hoping to see some encouragement, but there wasn't any. "What are our other options?"

"We can try and cast the injury. You will need to keep him confined to a stall to rest the leg and hope for the best. He's a calm fellow, so he may do well, but the recovery time will be much longer. The only other choice is to have him put down."

Captain Watson crossed his arms over his chest. "What will the surgery cost?"

Dr. Cutter's scowl turned into a look of sorrow. He said gently, "Around fifteen thousand dollars, depending on how well he does. Complications can raise the cost considerably. The clinic typically asks for half of the payment up front."

"That much?"

"Or more."

Lindsey's heart sank at the expression on her captain's face. She knew even before he spoke what he was going to say.

"I'm afraid the unit doesn't have a budget to cover a medical bill like that. We are just scraping by as it is."

"The costs for the cast and follow-up will be much less than the surgery. Is that the treatment you want us to use?"

Quickly, she said, "Couldn't we at least try to requisition the money?"

"Of course I will, but with the budget cuts we've had, I doubt command is going to give up that kind of money for a horse. I'm sorry, Sergeant, I know how much he means to you. Can he be transported back to the base, Doctor?"

"I'll need to keep him here for several weeks to make sure the cast doesn't need any adjustments and monitor his condition. After that, I'm sure the base vet can manage his care. We'll need follow up X-rays to make sure the leg is healing, but those can be done at your stable."

Captain Watson held out his hand. "Thank you, Dr. Cutter. We'll leave Dakota here until you think it's safe to move him."

Brian shook the offered hand. "Our equine services here at the Veterinarian Medical Teaching Hospital are among the finest in the world."

It was his standard line when clients were

worried about leaving their animals, but this time he was the one who was worried. The young woman was so pale he thought she might pass out at any moment. The horse must mean a great deal to her if she came straight from the hospital in her condition to check on him. Brian knew how much pain a broken bone caused.

She looked up. "Can I see him?"

"I'm not sure. You look like you need to lie down."

Rising, she faced him with determination blazing in her eyes. "I'm not leaving until I see him."

He looked to her captain, but all the man did was shrug and try to hold back a grin. Brian could tell he wasn't going to get any help from that direction. He shoved one hand into his lab coat pocket and nodded toward the door. "All right, but if you pass out, you'll just lie on the floor. I don't do humans."

"What a blessing for us," she shot back.

He turned away without voicing the comment on the tip of his tongue and led the way to the door beside the reception desk. She was stubborn, irritating and yet pathetic at the same time. So, why did he find her so attractive?

It made no sense. The sooner she saw her

horse, the sooner she would leave. Then maybe he could forget those beautiful eyes and the effect they seemed to have on his common sense.

He held open the door, but she stopped so close beside him that he could smell a subtle scent like peaches in her hair. He was tempted to lean closer to make sure. He didn't, when he realized how unprofessional it would appear.

"What do you think his chances are without surgery?" she asked in a low voice as she stared at him intently.

Such beautiful, sad, green eyes. How could he add to her sorrow? This was the part of his job he dreaded most. He glanced back at the other unit members. They were watching him intently. The words he needed to say stuck in his throat. He sought to give her some hope. "Every patient is different. Only time will tell."

"If he were your horse, what would you do?"

"If he were my horse and surgery wasn't an option?"

"Yes."

"I wouldn't let him suffer. I'd spend as much time as I needed saying goodbye, then I'd have him put down."

"No! I couldn't stand that." The last bit of

color leeched from her face. She turned away, and the sudden movement caused her to lose her balance. His cane clattered to the floor as he caught hold of her.

CHAPTER THREE

"Easy, I've got you." Brian held the slender form of the woman against his chest and struggled to keep upright for both their sakes.

Her hair did smell like peaches. Funny, he hadn't pictured her as the type of woman to use a scented shampoo. She struck him as a soldier through and through. It was intriguing to know she had a feminine side. He steadied himself by leaning back against the wall.

"I'm fine. It's just a dizzy spell," she said quickly.

The tight grip of her hand on his lab coat lapel told him more than words how much distress she was in. If there was one thing he knew well, it was the signs of pain — in animals and in humans.

A second later her fellow soldiers reached them. Shane swept Lindsey up into his arms without a moment's hesitation and Brian had no choice but to let him. Seeing how easily and gently the man lifted her made Brian acutely aware of his own physical shortcomings. Years ago he had carried Emily just as effortlessly. He thought he had come to terms with his disability a long time ago, but obviously he hadn't.

His limp was only a small reminder of the tragedy his carelessness had brought about. In one night he had lost both his wife and their unborn child. His mistake had cost him everything he held dear and he had only himself to blame.

Lee quickly retrieved Brian's cane and handed it to him. Taking the polished wooden staff, Brian nodded his thanks and ignored his feelings of inadequacy. He extended one hand indicating a door a few steps down the hall. "My office has a sofa in it. You can lay her down in there. Do you want me to call nine-one-one?"

"No." The weak murmur came from Lindsey.

"Are you sure?" Shane asked, looking uncertain.

She nodded as if more words were beyond her.

"This way," Brian said, and moved to open his door. Inside his office, he swept up a few papers and books from the brown leather sofa to make room for her.

Shane lowered her gingerly, then stood back. None of the men seemed to know what to do next. Brian cleared his throat. "Would you like a drink of water?"

"Yes, please," she whispered. She still hadn't opened her eyes.

Brian grabbed a paper cup from the dispenser on the wall and filled it from the bottled container beside it. Moving back to her side, he settled himself on the edge of the couch. He lifted her head and held the cup to her lips. She took a sip then sighed. He lowered her head back to the cushion.

She opened one eye. "I thought you didn't do humans."

"I make exceptions for women dressed in Civil War uniforms."

For an instant a smile tugged at the edge of her lips before she winced in pain again. "How fortunate can a girl get?"

"Are you sure you don't want me to call nine-one-one?"

"Two rides in an ambulance in one day would be more than my ego can take. I don't suppose you have some really good pain medicine handy. The pills they gave me at the hospital don't seem to be doing much."

"I've got a ton of good stuff here."

49

She opened both eyes. "Really?"

He nodded. "I've got drugs that will knock out a horse."

"Ha-ha. What does a girl have to do to get some?"

He was pleased to see her smile return, along with a bit more color in her cheeks. "She would need to grow two more legs and a tail."

"Are you telling me I don't measure up as one of your patients?"

"I never said anything of the kind. It's actually nice to be able to ask a patient where it hurts and get an answer."

"It hurts exactly where my horse landed on me."

"From my vantage point that looked like almost all of you."

"You are so right. If you aren't going to supply me with drugs, can you help me sit up?"

Brian didn't have a chance to help her. Her comrades were more than happy to oblige. He moved out of their way. When she was sitting upright she waved them aside. "I'm okay now. Don't hover."

The men backed up, but they didn't look ready to leave her to her own devices.

Brian filled the cup again with more water and handed it to her. To his relief, he saw that her color was almost back to normal. "If you won't go to the hospital, at least go home and lie on your own sofa so I can have mine back."

Taking the offered drink, she sipped it and nodded. "Once I see Dakota, I'll do just that."

All of the men began to protest together, but she ignored their scolding and stood. Cradling her arm, she winced but remained steady on her feet. "Show me the way, Dr. Cutter."

"He's down the hall, through the doors at the very end and in the first stall on the left."

He felt slightly cheated as he watched her fellow unit members guide her out the door, one on each side with her captain close behind. It wasn't that he wanted her to fall into his arms again. Of course not. He simply wanted to make sure she was all right. But that was what her friends wanted, too, he reminded himself. And they certainly had more of a right to care for her than he did. He was nothing but a stranger.

The thought brought back his frown. He was more than that. He was the man who might have to put her beloved horse to sleep.

Early Monday morning, Lindsey begged a ride to the Large Animal Clinic with Shane.

When they arrived, they saw Lee and Avery just going in. It seemed that all of them wanted to check on Dakota before they started their duties for the day.

As she approached Dakota's stall, Lindsey was surprised to see Captain Watson had arrived before them. He was deep in conversation with Dr. Cutter.

When her captain caught sight of them, he smiled. "I've been talking to the doctor and he has a way to do surgery on Dakota at a reduced cost to our unit."

Lindsey's heart jumped as happiness surged through her. "How is that possible?"

Dr. Cutter cleared his throat. "Using a new surgical procedure that I've developed — I told you about it the other day. Dakota's break is exactly the sort I'm hoping to trial this repair on."

"But you said it wasn't an option." Shane frowned at the doctor.

"I received notice of my grant acceptance this morning. It is an experimental procedure. If Dakota is entered in the study, it will mean I will have total control of his care. My fees and much of his care will be covered, but that will still leave the bill for his boarding and supplies that the army will have to pay. Unfortunately, the grant isn't a large one."

"We can raise the money if we have to," Captain Watson said.

"Absolutely," Avery chimed in. "He's one of our own. We won't let him down."

"Of course not," Lindsey added. She had a little in savings. She would gladly give the money to help pay for Dakota's care. "When you say experimental, Dr. Cutter, do you mean there is a chance that this won't help him?"

"There is that chance, but I have every confidence that he will do well. If my procedure works, he could be out of his cast in as little as six weeks."

Six weeks. That meant Dakota would be able to travel to Washington, D.C., in time for the Inaugural parade. Lindsey's joy danced like a soap bubble in the wind.

Thank you, God, for giving Dakota into the care of this man.

Captain Watson turned to Brian. "You have my permission to enroll Dakota in your study."

"Excellent. There are some forms you'll need to sign. If you'll follow me to my office, we can take care of that now."

When the two men walked away, Lindsey opened the gate and stepped into the stall where Dakota stood quietly. He rested with his head lowered and his eyes half-closed.

His dazed look worried her until she realized that they would be giving him pain medication and sedation to keep him quiet.

"Hey, Dakota. How's it going, fella?"

His head came up at the sound of her voice and he whinnied softly. Delighted at his responsiveness, she stepped closer and began to rub the side of his face. "Don't worry about a thing. Dr. Cutter is going to fix you up in no time."

Behind her, Avery said, "Do you think an experimental surgery using gene therapy is the best way to go?"

Shane moved up to stand beside Lindsey. Reaching out, he patted Dakota's neck. "It sounds a bit like science fiction to me."

"I have faith that it will work. I think the Lord brought us here at exactly the right time for Dakota to get this care."

Lee shoved his hands into his front pockets. "It would have been better if He had kept Dakota from breaking a leg in the first place."

Lindsey didn't answer. This, too, had to be part of God's plan, but like Danny's injury, it was a bitter pill to swallow.

She ran her hand over Dakota's soft nose. Her faith was being tested. The words of Psalm 9:9 echoed in her mind.

The Lord is a refuge for the oppressed, a

stronghold in times of trouble.

In her time of trouble, had she turned to the Lord as she should have? Perhaps that was what she was being shown. Little by little, she let go of the anger she had been holding on to.

I will try to listen with my heart for Your wisdom, Lord. Show me the path and I will do my best to travel it.

Three days later, Lindsey was struggling to use the can opener with her left hand when the doorbell rang. She stared at the container of corn that refused to fit in the opener. "We're not done. I won't be defeated by an inanimate object."

She noticed the faint smell of burning mozzarella, but the oven timer said her frozen pizza still had five minutes to go. The doorbell chimed again. Leaving the tiny kitchenette of her apartment, she crossed the living room to the front door. She opened it and stared in stunned silence.

"Surprise!" Her sister stood on the stoop with a suitcase resting beside her. Speechless, Lindsey could only stare.

Looking uncertain, Karen said, "Say something."

Shaking herself out of her stupor, Lindsey enfolded Karen in a one-armed hug. "Hello.

This certainly is a surprise. What are you doing here?"

Karen returned the embrace. "I'm just visiting."

Taking a step back, Lindsey studied Karen's face. Her sister had always been the rebel in the family. Her shaggy, cropped blond hair haloed a heart-shaped face. Danny often said Karen's big brown eyes and ready smile could make men weak in the knees, but her quirky wit was her greatest gift. Karen had a smile on her face now, but it didn't erase the sadness that lurked in the depths of her gaze.

"From the look on your face I'd say this is more than just visiting. What brings you all the way from Washington, D.C. to Kansas?"

"Invite me in and I'll tell you about it. Oh, you poor woman, look at you. You're covered in bruises."

"Having a horse roll over you will do that. Honestly, Karen, why are you here? Did Dad send you to take care of me?"

"No, although I'm sure he would have thought of it in a day or two," Karen added quickly.

"You should be helping Abigail and Danny. I can take care of myself."

Karen cleared her throat. "I just needed to get away for a while. I'm sorry I didn't call. Showing up and surprising you seemed like a good idea at the time, but it wasn't, was it?"

Lindsey reached out and took her hand. "It's a wonderful idea. You know I'm always happy to see you. Come in and tell me why you're here."

Karen's face brightened. "Later. You don't happen to have some tea, do you?"

"I'll tell you what. If you can wrestle open a can of corn for me, I'll make you a whole pot."

Inside the apartment, Karen followed Lindsey into the kitchen. At the entrance to the small room decorated with rooster wallpaper and rooster border above the few white cabinets, Karen paused and stared up at the large rooster-shaped clock on the wall. The avocado-green refrigerator began its noisy rumbling and Lindsey gave it a sharp shove to silence the sound. After a moment, Karen said in a tentative murmur, "You have a . . . nice place."

"Don't even try to be kind. It's a rental and it's cheap. I don't care what the wallpaper looks like as long as the roosters don't crow."

"What a marvelous attitude."

"I'm easy, what can I say?"

Karen wrinkled her nose. "I think something's burning."

"Oh, that's just my lunch. Can you help me with this? I damaged a nerve when I broke my arm and my hand is completely useless. I can't feel a thing." Handing her sister the offending can, Lindsey indicated the opener with a tilt of her head.

Karen's eyes widened in alarm. "Dad never mentioned that you had no feeling in your arm. Is it permanent?"

Lindsey rushed to reassure her, knowing she was thinking about Danny's condition. "No, the specialist said in two or three months I'll be as good as new. Dad didn't say anything because I haven't told him."

"Does this mean you won't be riding in the Inaugural parade?"

"I haven't given up hope. I've got two months and then some to recover."

"Lindsey, you should let the family know you might not be there. Everyone is making plans to attend."

"By everyone, I assume you mean Danny, too?"

"It's all he talks about to the nurses and therapists who come to the house. He is so proud of you. He insists he'll be there to watch you and Dakota in person."

"Now you know why I don't have the heart to say anything yet."

"Yes, I guess I do," Karen said softly.

Lindsey hesitated. "There's more."

"What?"

"Dakota broke a bone in his front leg when we fell."

"Oh, no!"

"He's had surgery and we think he is going to be fine."

Karen pressed a hand to her forehead. "No wonder Abigail thought there was something you weren't telling us the last time you called."

"I didn't want to keep secrets, but I wanted to be sure of things one way or the other before I gave Danny that news."

"Are you sure of things now?"

"Not really."

"Lindsey, you have to tell him. Danny is stronger than you think. If you could only see the way he tackles his therapy sessions. He's able to raise his right shoulder now and he's up to almost two hours off his ventilator each day."

"He's working hard because he has a goal to reach. That is exactly why I'm not going to tell him yet. I can't risk taking away his motivation. I have faith that Dakota and I will both be in Washington, D.C., and Danny will be strong enough to be there to see it."

"I don't agree with you, but I won't say anything for now."

"That's all I'm asking. Thank you. So, are you going to open that can for me or not?"

Smiling, her sister tossed the can in the air and caught it again. "I'll give it my best shot."

Karen successfully extracted the yellow kernels from their stubborn metal prison while Lindsey put the kettle on to boil. A minute later the oven timer rang. Karen snatched up the pot holder before Lindsey could reach it and opened the oven. She pulled out a cookie sheet with a small pizza on it.

"This is your lunch?"

"That and the corn."

"Pizza and corn?"

"It's not as weird as it sounds."

"Yes, it is. You need something healthy." Karen set the cookie sheet on top of the stove.

"This is healthy."

"At least drink some milk with it." Karen pulled open the refrigerator door.

Lindsey winced. She knew there wasn't any milk. In fact, there wasn't much of anything in her fridge except a half-empty bottle of ketchup and one lonely dill pickle in a jar. "I haven't had a chance to get to the commissary."

Karen shut the door and frowned at Lindsey. "Since when?"

"Since before the accident."

"Obviously, it's a good thing I stopped by. Eat while I have a cup of tea and then I'll drive you to wherever you need to go."

Lindsey used a spatula to transfer her overly crisp pizza to a plate and then set the plate on the table. "You don't have to run errands for me."

"I can see that no one else is. Where are the tea bags?"

The kettle began to whistle. After finding a cup and filling it with hot water, Karen joined Lindsey at the table. Waiting until after her sister had fixed the tea, Lindsey asked, "Are you going to tell me why you're here?"

Karen raised her cup to her lips and blew on the steaming brew. She took a sip and set the cup down. "This is very good tea. What kind did you say it was?"

"Earl Grey, and don't change the subject."

Taking a deep breath, Karen closed her eyes and said, "It's Dad."

"I don't understand."

Karen leaned her elbows on the table. "He won't stop fixing me up. I'm only twenty-one but all of the sudden he acts like I'm the only chance he'll ever have for grand-children. There has been a steady parade of guys who just *happen* to stop by our apartment. He's driving me crazy."

"I'm sure Dad — like the rest of us — is having a hard time adjusting to Danny's condition. Do you want me to talk to him?" Lindsey took one bite of her pizza, then pushed the unappetizing concoction to the side.

"Thanks for the offer," Karen said gently. "But I'm hoping a little separation will be good for both of us. That's why I'm at your door begging to stay and nurse you through this injury. And before you say no, I did discuss this with Abigail. She can do without me for a few weeks. Please, can I stay?"

Lindsey patted the orthopedic brace and sling the specialist had fitted her with. "I don't need a nurse, but a roommate who can grocery shop and run the can opener will be a welcome addition until I'm out of this contraption."

"Honey, that sounds great." Karen's relief was evident.

"Don't be too sure. This is a one-bedroom apartment and that means *you* get the sofa."

Karen's tinkling laughter was music to Lindsey's ears. During their frequent and lengthy phone conversations, the sound of happiness had been sadly lacking in her sister's voice. Danny's injury had affected everyone. They were all trying to find a new "normal" for the family.

Picking up her teacup, Karen said, "Roommates pay rent. What's space on a lumpy couch going to cost me?"

"The use of two good arms and your skill as a chauffeur. If you really don't mind driving me, I'm dying to get over to the university to see how Dakota is doing. But what about school? Can you afford to take the time off?"

Setting the white cup down, Karen picked up her spoon and began to stir. "I had already decided to take a semester off. I couldn't concentrate in class. There was no use flunking out on top of everything else."

Seeing Karen's grief made Lindsey acutely aware that her baby sister was dealing with a lot more than their father's matchmaking. "I wish I was closer so that I could help, too."

Rising, she carried her plate to the counter. After dumping the remains of her uneaten lunch in the trash, she laid the dish in the sink and turned on the water. It was then that she felt Karen's hands on her shoulders turning her around.

Tears blurred Lindsey's vision and she

loathed the fact. She had tried so hard not to cry. "I hate that this has happened to him."

"I know." Karen's voice was low and brimming with emotion. "But Danny believed that protecting his country was more than a job. It was something that he knew in his heart he had to do."

Lindsey squeezed her eyes shut against the pain that swallowed her heart and made it hard to breathe. "But the price . . . was too high. He is the best . . . and the brightest . . . and this seems so cruel." The words, when she finally managed them, were ragged and broken between her sobs.

"I know you love him. He knows it, too."

"I haven't told him that often enough."

"You don't have to. He sees it. I wish I could hug you, but I'm afraid I'll hurt you."

"My left side is fine," she hiccupped. To prove it, she embraced Karen with one arm and the two of them clung together as they wept.

From the corner of his eye, Brian caught the fugitive movement. Without looking up from the grant application on his desk, he said, "Isabella, don't chew on that pencil."

The culprit ignored him.

He tried injecting more menace into his

tone. "Isabella, I said, no!"

The oversize brown lop-eared rabbit perched on the corner of his large desk chose to disregard his warning. She pulled her prize from the purple Wildcat mug he used to hold his writing utensils. Settling the yellow number two under one paw, she began to nibble it to bits.

"You little minx." He rose from his chair and scooped her up, tucking her firmly under one arm. He stuck the pencil back in the mug with numerous other scarred victims.

He drew a hand down her soft, furry body, then scratched her favorite spot behind her left ear. "Why do you always zero in on the new ones?"

Lifting his cane from the back of his chair, he crossed the office and pulled open the door. Seated at the reception desk was one of the young students who doubled as a part-time secretary for him.

"Jennifer, will you put Isabella in her outside cage, please?"

"Of course. What did you do to get banished from Dr. Cutter's desk this time?" she asked the rabbit as she took her from Brian.

"The usual," he answered.

"Ah, pencil nibbling, were we?" She, too, scratched the bunny behind the ears.

"I can't break her of the habit."

"You could try switching to pens."

"I like pencils. They let me change my mind as often as I need to."

"So does the delete key on your computer."

"It isn't the same."

Rolling her eyes, Jennifer headed for the outside door and said, "Therein lies your problem, Doctor. You have to learn to say what you mean the first time."

Brian turned back to his office. He knew how to say what he meant, but he was often accused of being too gruff. Whenever he needed to draft a letter or a grant application, he worked and reworked the words until they seemed soft and polite enough. Pencils worked best for the task. After he had the tone he wanted, he typed his work into his computer. Some might say he was making twice the work for himself, but he still preferred his tried-and-true method.

Certainly, his upcoming lecture on pastern arthrodesis for the Equine Surgical Conference in January was no exception. It was an honor to be asked to speak and he wanted his address to be perfect. He intended to rework it until he was completely satisfied. Fortunately, the college bookstore had an excellent supply of the large yellow legal pads he liked best.

Back at his desk, he put aside his work on his presentation for the moment and opened the file on Dakota. The gelding wasn't doing as well as he had hoped. The surgery itself had gone well, but the big horse seemed to be having more pain instead of less. That wasn't encouraging. A knock at his door caused him to look up. Jennifer stood in the doorway minus the rabbit.

She motioned toward the folder he held. "Is that the file on the army horse? I was wondering how he was getting along."

"I'm not happy with his progress. Even with the medication he's getting, his respiratory rate and pulse rate are higher than they should be. The staff has been reporting that he's restless and he isn't eating well."

"None of those are good signs."

A smile twitched at the corners of his mouth, but he held it back. "So you *have* been paying attention in class. Will wonders never cease?"

She blushed and looked chagrined. "Is there anything else you need, Doctor? If not, I'm going to take off."

He hadn't meant to offend her, but before he could form the right words to apologize, she was out the door.

Of all the females he had known in his

life, only Isabella never seemed to care what tone he chose or how gruff his words sounded. If only more women had her tolerance, his life would be a lot easier.

Before he had a chance to dwell on the current poor state of his interpersonal skills, Jennifer opened the door again. "Doctor, Sergeant Mandel is here to see you."

The sudden rush of pleasure he felt at hearing her name unnerved him. He tried unsuccessfully to stifle his excitement.

"Show her in."

"Yes, Doctor."

She nodded but before she could close the door, he said, "Jennifer, I was teasing earlier when I made that remark about you paying attention in class."

"You were?"

"Of course. I think you have an excellent future in the surgical field."

She looked doubtful. "You do?"

"I do."

She flipped her long blond hair back over one shoulder. "Wow! Okay, but next time you're kidding someone, Doc, you should smile."

"I'll certainly try to do so."

CHAPTER FOUR

Jennifer held open the door so that Lindsey and another young woman could enter Brian's office. Lindsey appeared much more rested today, he noticed when she walked in. To his surprise, she looked even prettier than he remembered. She radiated an energy that seemed to warm a place inside him that he had almost forgotten existed. Like the dancing flames of a campfire on a cold night in the mountains, she left him longing to draw closer to the warmth.

Wearing a camouflage shirt and matching pants with black boots, she looked every inch the soldier — except for the blue sling on her arm. She certainly wasn't the type of woman that normally would have interested him. Since his wife's death he couldn't think of a single woman he had been this attracted to, but there was something about this woman that intrigued him. He didn't care for the sensation. When he realized he was staring, he shook off the fanciful notion and rose to his feet. "Please come in, Sergeant Mandel. Have a seat."

Her smile flashed briefly and was gone. She appeared hesitant as she sat on the sofa. "Thank you for seeing us. This is my sister, Karen Mandel."

He nodded to the woman dressed in jeans and a tailored navy shirt. "I'm pleased to meet you."

Addressing the two of them, he said, "As you may know, Dakota's surgery went very well. He's tolerating his cast, which is always a good thing. In two to three weeks he'll go back to surgery to have the pins removed and a new cast applied."

"Yes, Captain Watson has been keeping us informed," Karen said softly.

"Captain Watson is the reason we're here," Lindsey began. "Because of this arm, I've been reassigned to light duty. My orders are to oversee Dakota's care."

"I don't understand."

"I'll be doing what I can to help here. Karen has asked to be involved, as well, and Captain Watson has agreed. Providing we're not in the way, of course."

"Are you sure you're fit to work?"

"I can do whatever is needed, within reason."

"Working around sick and injured horses can be dangerous."

She leaned toward him, her smile changing from hesitant to forced. "I know that, Doctor."

Of course she did. She was the one with the broken arm. Retreating into his most professional demeanor, he said tersely, "That is something you can't forget when you are here. Given your injury, I'm not sure what you will be able to do."

Her smile disappeared. Did he only imagine the room grew a few degrees cooler?

"I've been taking care of the unit's animals for over a year, Doctor. All sixteen horses plus the two mules. I'm sure I can manage to be of some help to you and your staff, even if all I do is muck out the stall. I know how to follow orders."

He sat back in his chair, registering her annoyed tone. She was upset, but he didn't know why. "Very well. I'll let the staff know that you'll be . . . assisting here until the horse is fit to return to the army's stables."

"Thank you," she snapped back.

"May I see Dakota now?" Karen asked, glancing between Lindsey and himself with an odd gleam in her eyes.

"Certainly. He is through the double doors at the end of the hallway. His stall is the first one on the left down the first aisle. I need to speak with my secretary and then I'll join you at his stall in case you have any questions."

Brian tucked the file under his arm and escaped from his office. Fortunately, Jennifer had already left for the evening. He laid the file down and raked his fingers through his hair as he tried to gather his scattered thoughts.

The idea of having Lindsey in the clinic every day was a disturbing one. Without understanding exactly why, he knew she would interfere with his work. She would be a distraction he didn't need, but he couldn't see how to prevent her from coming.

Her request wasn't all that unusual. Animal owners occasionally spent long hours with their pets and he'd rarely had to forbid access. Besides, she had her orders. There wasn't much he could do about it except try to avoid her.

Even as the thought occurred to him, he knew that avoiding Lindsey wasn't what he really wanted.

"Take a deep breath, Lindsey," Karen said after Dr. Cutter had left the room.

Lindsey tried to swallow her irritation with the man. "I'm a soldier in the United States

Army. I've been trained to do my duty no matter what the circumstances. A broken arm is no treat, but I've been assigned to Dakota's care and I'll follow my orders. It doesn't matter if he thinks I can or not."

"He's only trying to be kind."

"I didn't hear a lick of kindness in his tone."

"Maybe not in his tone, but I certainly saw it in the way he was looking at you."

Lindsey turned to Karen in stunned surprise. "You've got to be kidding."

"I don't blame you for being interested in him. He's attractive and he loves animals — what's not to like?"

"I certainly don't see the same thing you do. Come on, I'll show you where they're keeping Dakota."

Leaving his office, Lindsey glanced toward the reception area. Dr. Cutter was standing at the desk, but his cute young secretary was nowhere to be seen. Not that it mattered what his hired help looked like. It certainly didn't matter. Not to her, Lindsey decided.

Leading Karen toward the recovery stalls, Lindsey waited until they were through the door before she spoke her mind.

"The man is rude and he's arrogant and I am certainly not interested in him."

"I'll admit he needs a little fine-tuning, but he has potential."

"Potential for what? No, don't tell me or you'll sound like Danny. He never lets up with the 'When are you going to settle down?' speech. Once he got married, all he could think about was how I needed to find someone, too."

Being in love had made him forget the painful scenes from their childhood, but Lindsey never forgot them. She knew better than to believe she could make an army career and a marriage work. Her own parents had been perfect examples of how wrong it could get. The endless fights, the recriminations, the tears and the broken promises she had witnessed as a child were things she couldn't forget. As far as she was concerned, it was better not to have children than to subject them to the kind of childhood she'd had.

Marriage was hard enough without adding frequent reassignment, long separations and dangerous duty to the mix. Danny had been willing to take the chance that he could make it work with Abigail, and maybe they would be one of the blessed ones, but Lindsey wasn't willing to open her heart up to that kind of pain.

At Dakota's stall, Karen leaned through

the rails and ran a hand down the big bay's nose. "Whatever made you think I was talking about settling down?" she quipped. The sly smile she cast Lindsey over her shoulder made Lindsey want to shake her.

Leaning on the gate beside her sister, Lindsey decided to set her straight. "For your information, I have no intention of starting a relationship. The army is my life. I love moving to new posts, seeing new places, meeting new people."

"Why? I hated it as a kid."

"I guess the good Lord gave me the wanderlust gene. Our father had it and the next generation of Mandels will probably have it, too."

"Except that there won't be a next generation of Mandels." Karen's soft words brought the extent of their loss into sharp focus.

Lindsey slipped her good arm over Karen's shoulders. "I'm sorry. That was a thoughtless comment on my part. We can pray that Danny and Abigail may still be blessed with a child."

"I guess we can't spend our lives trying not to say or do something that will remind us of Danny's condition. I think it has been hardest on Dad. He really wanted to see the traditions of the family carried on."

"I know. That's my duty now. I'm going to carry on and serve with distinction."

"Why? Hasn't our family given this country enough?"

"You don't mean that."

"I've often wondered if you aren't trying to live the life you think Dad wanted without finding out what kind of life you wanted for yourself."

"This *is* the life I want," Lindsey insisted.

Karen sighed in defeat. "As long as that's true then I'm going to be happy for you, but you don't have to do it alone. Sharing life's burdens is part of the reason God made it so that two could become one."

Reaching out, Lindsey tweaked her sister's nose. "When did you get so wise?"

"I think it was in Philosophy 101 my freshman year."

Lindsey smiled at her joke. The door to the hallway opened and Brian walked over to join them. "Do you have any questions, ladies?"

Lindsey turned to study Dakota. The cast extended from above his knee to below his hoof. It was wrapped in bright blue cloth.

"As you can see," Brian began, "he is wearing special shoes on his other feet to accommodate the height of the cast and keep him standing level."

76

"Why is that important?" Karen stepped over to make room for Brian to stand between herself and Lindsey.

"It will help prevent undue stress on his other legs. Horses carry most of their weight on their front legs. Unlike dogs or cats, they can't stand three legged for long. We want him standing evenly, but not moving around much."

"I expected to see him hanging from a sling."

"We do use slings if we have to, but usually that is for bone breaks in the upper legs."

Lindsey drew her hand down Dakota's neck. "He doesn't look as if he feels well. Is he in pain?"

Brian flipped through the chart that was wired to the front of the stall. "I've ordered pain medication. He's been receiving regular doses. His X-rays show the pins are in excellent position. He should recover full use of the leg."

Lindsey finally voiced the question she had been afraid to ask until now. "Do you believe Dakota could be healed enough to walk three miles with a rider by late January?"

"It might be possible, but I can't give you a guarantee."

"He has to be fit by then. If it's possible, then that's good enough for me. If you do your best for him, prayer will take us the rest of the way."

"I'm sorry, but why does he have to be fit by late January?"

She turned to face him. "Because the Commanding General's Mounted Color Guard will be participating in the Inaugural Parade in Washington, D.C., on January twentieth and Dakota has to be there."

Brian shook his head. "That's only ten weeks away."

"But is it possible?"

"If this new treatment works as well as I hope, perhaps, but you certainly can't count on it."

"He'll make it. I know he will. I have faith."

"Unrealistic expectations will only lead to disappointment, Sergeant Mandel."

"Aren't you a man of faith?" Karen asked.

"I'm a man of science, especially when I'm in this building. Dakota's progress will be carefully documented and analyzed to help gauge the success or failure of this therapy. I believe in what can be documented. I believe in results that I can quantify."

Lindsey studied his face and noticed again

78

the stormy gray color of his eyes. Was he always so serious, she wondered? What did he do for fun? Was he married? She glanced at his hand. He didn't wear a ring.

The direction her speculations were heading surprised her. She forced herself to stick to the important topic at hand. "Has this therapy been tried before?"

"In small animals like rabbits and dogs, but surgical repairs on horses are very different. Their weight is the biggest issue. The stress load on the healing break can be very high. That can lead to repair failures, especially if the horse is high-strung and doesn't remain quiet."

"Dakota isn't high-strung, but he loves to work. I'm not sure how he'll take being confined."

"He has been quiet for us."

Lindsey ran a hand down Dakota's back. "I still think he is in pain. Isn't there something else you can do for him?"

"I don't want to add additional medications unless I have to. If he is having pain, I'm sure it will decrease soon."

Lindsey noticed that Brian seemed ill at ease. He didn't make eye contact with her. He kept a tight grip on the chart as if it was some type of shield. His superior manner began to irritate her. Either he wasn't really concerned about the horse or he didn't think she knew what she was talking about. Why did everything this man said rub her the wrong way?

"It isn't fair that Dakota has to suffer because you don't want to mess up your study."

"I assure you we don't let our patients suffer needlessly."

"How can I be sure of that?"

His eyebrows shot up in surprise. "Are you questioning my judgment?"

"Of course not, Dr. Cutter," Karen interjected calmly. "I'm sure Dakota is getting the best of care."

"He is. If you intend to make yourself useful, Sergeant, I suggest you see my secretary first thing in the morning. She will supply you with a list of duties and the times we have set up for Dakota's treatments. I'm sure she'll be able to find something you can manage with one arm."

With that, he left the two women and exited through an outside door.

Lindsey cast a sideways glance at Karen. "You're right, he has potential. He has the potential to annoy me to no end. He isn't the only one who knows about horses. There's more than one way to treat pain in an animal."

"You aren't giving him a chance, Lindsey."

Maybe Karen was right. "I know, but something about him gets to me."

"Why?"

"Maybe it's because he never smiles. When he's talking to me, I get the feeling that he'd rather be somewhere else. Maybe I just don't like that he was right and I was wrong the day Dakota fell."

Karen studied Lindsey for a long moment. "I think there is more to your feeling than dislike. You know, I think I'm going to enjoy watching the two of you butt heads."

As he pulled into the driveway of his home, Brian decided he had wasted enough time thinking about Lindsey Mandel. Why should he care if she didn't trust his judgment? Except that he did care.

Stepping out of his pickup, he opened the small carrier on the front seat that Isabella rode in and lifted her out. "Come on, girl, we're home. Let's see what the mailman left for us."

With Isabella tucked under one arm, he made his way up the walk to a small white cottage with dark blue shutters. The house stood on a tall hilltop overlooking the Kansas River as it wound its way eastward out of the plains and through the rolling hills of eastern Kansas before it emptied into the wider Missouri River near Kansas City.

The view was one of the reasons he'd purchased the place. It reminded him a little of the view from his parent's home in Montana. Although the Kansas hills didn't compare to the foothills of the Bighorn Range, the view and the smell of the tall cedars and pine trees beside the front door always took him back to the mountains — back to where he and Emily had been so happy together. He let the grief pour out now that he was alone. The ache in his heart had become a part of him. It never left.

From the brass mailbox, he extracted a handful of envelopes and flyers. "Looks like you're in luck, Isabella. There's lots of junk mail."

He tucked his mail under his chin as he struggled to unlock the door without dropping the rabbit, the correspondences or his cane. Once inside, he closed the door, then set his pet on the floor. She scampered to a box beside his chair and hopped in.

Brian crossed the hardwood floor and sank with a sigh of relief into his recliner. He rubbed his thigh for a minute before leaning back and raising the leg cushion. From the table beside him, he picked up a silver-framed photo. In it his wife, Emily, smiled sweetly back at him. He had taken the picture of her when they were on their honeymoon. It had been her favorite.

"You wouldn't believe the day I've had," he began. "My newest patient has the most irritating owner."

He often told Emily about the challenges of his job, but tonight he found he didn't want to tell her about Lindsey. It didn't seem right.

The silence of the house closed in, filling him with an aching sense of loss that never faded. He didn't deserve to have it fade. He had killed the woman he loved and nothing would ever change that fact.

He set the picture aside and picked up his mail. Sorting through it with Isabella was also a nightly ritual. The flyers from the local grocery stores he tossed into the box with the rabbit. She instantly began to shred them into pieces. Next to nibbling pencils, paper shredding was her favorite pastime and one he allowed her to indulge in only in her special plastic bin.

It hadn't taken him long to learn that a bored rabbit could be very destructive. He'd had to replace the wooden handle on his recliner twice during the first year Isabella lived with him. Fortunately, he had discovered the cure before any other items of furniture had to be replaced. If he gave her something fun to do, she was as good as gold.

He turned over the first envelope. "Hey, we might have won ten million dollars. It says all we have to do is enter to win. Like that will happen."

He crumpled the envelope and contents and tossed it into the box. Isabella attacked the new paper with glee. The next two envelopes were bills. He considered tossing them in with the rabbit, but decided against it. Telling the electric company that his rabbit had ripped up the bill wasn't likely to keep the lights on if he missed a payment. The third envelope bore the logo of the United Jockey Club Research Foundation. Knowing the UJC Research Foundation had donated nearly one million dollars in grants the previous year, he quickly tore open the letter.

"Listen to this, Isabella. They are interested in my new study. They're calling it groundbreaking work and their grant committee is interested in learning more. They plan on sending a representative to hear my presentation and review my data at the Equine Surgical Conference in January."

Brian glanced at his pet, but she was only

interested in her game. Picking up Emily's picture, he studied the face he knew so well.

"Do you know what this means, honey? If they back my project, I won't have to beg money and cut corners to make ends meet at the clinic for years."

Things were falling into place for his work. The conference would bring the best and brightest equine surgeons in North America to hear him, along with a dozen other speakers. If he could persuade Equine Equipment to have one of their ambulances on display he might be able to convince the college advisory board to actively pursue purchasing one for the clinic. Just the thought of the horses who could be saved by being safely transported to the clinic brought a lump to his throat.

He held Emily's picture close to his heart. "I wish you were here to share this with me."

After a while, the unshed tears stopped stinging the back of his eyes. Little by little, the silence of the house lulled him into sleep. As he did almost every night, he fell asleep in the chair with Emily's face pressed to his chest and her presence filling his dreams.

Sometime later, Brian awoke with a start. He had been dreaming, but not about his wife. The woman he saw riding toward him on a bay horse had had red hair and green eyes. Disgusted with himself for letting Lindsey intrude into his personal life, he got up and put Isabella in her cage before making his way to his bedroom.

Sleep was a long time in coming. When it did arrive, he dreamed about his childhood — about lying on his back and looking up through the green aspen leaves and feeling the whole world was full of promise. Green leaves that were the same color as Lindsey's beguiling eyes.

Early the next morning, Brian walked into the entrance of the Large Animal Clinic with a half-formed plan for the day. Isabella lay firmly tucked in the crook of his arm. He hadn't slept well and he was sure it showed. Thoughts of Lindsey had kept him up until long into the night.

Why on earth he couldn't stop thinking about her was something he couldn't understand. And she was going to be here again today. The plan he had come up with for dealing with her was to make rounds as early as possible and then barricade himself in his office. It wasn't much of a plan, but it was all he could come up with at three-thirty in the morning. Looking up, he was surprised to see Jennifer crossing the room quickly to meet him.

"Good morning, Dr. Cutter. Let me take Isabella outside for you."

"Thank you, but I'd like to have her with me in the office today." He had a feeling he was going to need her comforting presence to help keep him on track and not think about Lindsey. Sergeant Mandel, he corrected himself.

Jennifer gave him a tight smile and took Isabella out of his arms. "I'm just going to take her anyway. You know how loud voices upset her."

"Not that I've ever noticed." Puzzled, he tried to make sense of Jennifer's tense demeanor. "Are you planning on yelling at me? Whatever I did, I apologize."

Gathering the oversize rabbit into her arms, Jennifer said, "It's not something *you* did."

"I'm glad to hear that. Oh, before I forget, Sergeant Mandel is going to be in today. Give her a list of her horse's treatments and let her do what she can to help."

Jennifer's look held a trace of pity. "She's already here. I'm just going to be outside with Isabella for a while."

With the rabbit in her arms, Jennifer hurried out the door.

Shrugging off her peculiar behavior, Brian

limped toward his office. So Lindsey was here already. That shot down the first stage of his plan. He would certainly encounter her when he made rounds. As he was unlocking his door, two of the fourth-year students came down the hall from the holding area. They stopped short at the sight of him, then hurried past with their heads down. He glanced after them with a puzzled frown. What was going on? Whatever it was, he wasn't ready to face it until he had at least one cup of coffee.

Inside his office, he set out the carpet-covered boxes Isabella used as steps to reach the top of his desk and her favorite spot — an old towel in a shallow tray at the far corner. After starting the coffee, he held his cup under the brewer until it was full, then slipped in the pot. The first sip of the scalding hot, dark brew was exactly what he needed. Taking a second sip, he set the cup on his desk, put on his lab coat and headed down the hall to check on his patients.

The first thing he noticed when he entered the stall area was the large group of students clustered outside Dakota's stall. He hurried forward. If something had gone wrong and he hadn't been called, heads were going to roll.

CHAPTER FIVE

"What's going on here?" Brian's irate bellow caused the students hovering outside Dakota's stall to part like the waters of the Red Sea.

Lindsey winked at the elderly woman inserting hair-fine acupuncture needles along the horse's neck and turned to face the oncoming battle. She even managed to put on her sweetest smile. "Good morning, Dr. Cutter."

"What is the meaning of this?"

"Allow me to introduce Mia Chang. She is a horse acupuncturist."

"I can see that. What is she doing with my patient?"

"I am relieving his pain and the great stress he is suffering from," Mia said with a slight bow in Brian's direction before turning her attention back to Dakota.

"It's quite remarkable, actually," one of the students ventured. "His pulse and respirations are back to normal and he has a brighter look in his eyes after only twenty minutes of therapy."

"Yes, he is feeling much better. This will help strengthen the healing bones." Mia pulled a handful of pellets from her pocket and held them under Dakota's nose. He nibbled them up with relish.

"What is that?" another student asked.

"My special blend of healing herbs with a little honey to sweeten the taste. I can give you the recipe if you like."

Lindsey didn't think Brian's scowl could get any deeper, but it did. He leaned forward on his cane. "Ms. Mandel, may I speak to you privately in my office?"

His cold, clipped words told Lindsey not to expect a thank-you. He turned and left without waiting for her answer. She followed him down the hall, fully prepared to fight for Dakota's well-being. It was obvious that the horse was feeling better and she wasn't about to let Dr. Grumpy change that.

Inside his office, he indicated she should take a seat. She preferred to stand, but the thought that he might be uncomfortable or in pain standing made her hasten to sit on the sofa. She wondered what the carpeted boxes stacked up beside his desk were for but decided not to ask.

Brian sat with a tiny sigh of relief that made her glad she hadn't insisted on confronting him while he was on his feet. Knowing that the best defense was a good offence, she launched into her prepared speech. "I'm sure you're happy Dakota is obviously in less pain. I'm certainly glad Miss Chang was able to come on such short notice."

"Sergeant Mandel —"

"Her techniques have worked wonders with some of our other horses. My father was stationed in South Korea when I was ten and I saw firsthand the value of their nontraditional medicine."

"I appreciate your desire to help your horse, but —"

"I knew you would. That's why I asked her to come. She is also a trained veterinary assistant."

"Miss Mandel —"

"Her fee will be covered by me personally, so you don't need to worry about that."

"Lindsey, please."

The husky way he said her first name sent an unexpected shiver along her nerve endings and blotted all other comments from her mind. She waited in silence for his next words. For a heartbeat he simply stared into her eyes and she wondered what he was thinking.

He looked down and took a deep breath. When he looked up again he didn't appear angry, just tired. She had the craziest urge to take his hand and offer him comfort or at least a cup of hot tea.

"Lindsey, do you know how many horses are put down each year in this country for a simple fracture of the leg? I don't mean just the expensive racehorses or show horses, but horses that belong to ordinary people who love them?"

"No."

"Hundreds. Maybe even thousands. I've euthanized far too many of them myself. Do you know why I put most of them down?"

"Because the breaks can't be healed?"

He shook his head. "No. It would be easier to take if that were true. Money is the single biggest reason a horse gets put to sleep. The average person simply can't afford to spend fifteen thousand dollars on an animal's medical care. But what if that cost could be cut in half?"

"More horses could be saved?" she ventured, feeling less in the right with each passing minute.

"Maybe hundreds more each year. That is what I'm trying to do with the study Dakota is in. I'm trying to prove this therapy will cut healing time and therefore the cost of a break significantly. But to do that I have to have absolute hard facts. Facts that can be reproduced in other horses time after time. Facts that can be published in a reputable journal."

She listened to him with a sinking sensation. "You're trying to tell me I've altered the study."

"I'm trying to make you understand how important this work is. I don't want to see your horse in pain any more than you do. But I have to know that what I give him to help won't interfere with what I'm trying to accomplish."

"I don't see how simple acupuncture can interfere with your gene therapy."

"In all likelihood it won't. But what if he begins to run a fever? What if the herbs he ate today react with the antibiotics I have to give him? Just because a substance is a natural remedy doesn't mean it can't have side effects. The fewer variables I have to deal with, the better."

"I understand what you're saying. I wasn't thinking about how important Dakota's recovery will be for others. I was only thinking of how important it is for me. I'm sorry if I've interfered with your work."

She looked so contrite that Brian was tempted to smile. "I want your help and input. All I'm asking is that you discuss your ideas with me first. Can I have your promise on that?"

Nodding, she said, "Of course."

"Good. This is a teaching hospital and acupuncture is gaining ground as a legitimate treatment for pain and lameness in horses. The students seemed quite interested in Miss Chang's techniques. I may see about including her in our guest lecture series next semester."

"She would like that."

The sudden silence between them seemed weighted with tension and expectation.

"Will you be staying long today?" he asked, not wanting to see her leave in spite of his earlier plan.

"I have to get back to the post. Karen and I are helping organize a fund-raiser for the cost of Dakota's care that isn't going to be covered by your grant. The men and women at the fort have been overwhelming in their offers of support. We've already raised nearly a thousand dollars just with donations from the troops and their families."

"That's amazing."

"Dakota is an army horse. He's no different than any other injured soldier. We take

94

care of our own."

"I'll see you tomorrow then."

"Tomorrow our unit is traveling to Medicine Falls for their centennial celebration. I'm on restricted duty so I won't be riding, but I'm going along to help the ground crew and do the PR part of the job."

"PR?"

"People are always curious about the unit. We are ambassadors for the army, as well as a living history exhibition. We put on a really good show if you ever get the chance to see it."

She rose to her feet. Brian headed for the door and held it open for her. "If you need any help with the fund-raising, please don't hesitate to call me."

Brian could hardly believe what he heard himself saying. The words were out of his mouth before he even had a chance to consider the ramifications. He didn't get involved in the lives of the people who brought their animals to him. He certainly had no intention of getting involved with someone as impulsive and outspoken as this woman. His life was quiet and orderly. It was exactly the way he wanted it. At least it had been until he arrived at work this morning.

Lindsey cocked her head to the side and

grinned at him. "Thank you. I may take you up on that offer."

As she walked out the door, he realized with a sinking sensation that she might do just that.

Ten minutes later he looked up from his work at the sound of a timid knock. The door opened and Jennifer peeked in. "Is it safe to bring Isabella in?"

"For her, but maybe not for you."

She pushed the door open and stepped in with his pet draped over her arm. "Why? What did I do?"

"You took off faster than the proverbial rabbit at the first sign of trouble. I'd like to remind you that you work for me. The next time there's trouble brewing in this office, I expect you to be the first one to inform me of it."

"Was there trouble this morning?" she asked, giving him a wide-eyed innocent stare.

He glared back at her, but she simply put Isabella on the floor. The rabbit made a beeline for the steps he'd set out and quickly climbed to his desk. She paused in front of him long enough to have her head stroked, then she hopped to the far corner and settled herself in her favorite spot.

"I like Sergeant Mandel, don't you?" Jennifer asked, still lounging in the doorway.

He felt the heat of a blush creeping up his neck. "I haven't given it much thought."

"You spent a long time with her in here this morning."

"We were discussing Dakota's plan of care."

"I just noticed that the two of you seem to be getting along rather well when she left."

"Because we weren't shouting at each other?"

"That was my first clue, but I think it was your offer to help with fund-raising that clinched the deal. Is she married?"

"That is none of our business. She is a client."

"She's a cute client, even if she does wear combat boots. Don't you think so?"

Exasperated with her prying, he said, "Is there something you wanted, Jennifer?"

"Oh, right. The people who make that horse ambulance are on line one. I knew you'd been waiting for their call."

He picked up his phone, but hesitated before pressing the blinking button. It was his hope that he could convince Equine Enterprises to allow the school the use of one of their new ambulances for an extended period of time. The need to transport injured horses safely was no different than the need to transport people. He wanted to raise awareness of the issue and hopefully convince the school's board to purchase one. His first challenge would be to persuade Equine Enterprises to loan him the vehicle, only *his* PR skills weren't the best.

The image of Lindsey pressing his case popped into his mind. *She* was a persuasive person. She would be hard to stop when she had her mind set on something.

"Do you need anything else, Doctor?" Jennifer asked.

"No, thank you. Oh, wait. How far away is Medicine Falls?"

"It's about an hour northwest of here."

"Can you pull up a map on your computer?"

"Yes," she drawled. "But why would you want to go to Medicine Falls?"

That was a very good question, and one he wasn't sure he knew the answer to, except that Lindsey would be there.

"I have Saturday off. I heard they were having their centennial celebration. I thought I might take a drive up that way."

As answers went it was pretty weak, but it was the best he could do on the spur of the moment.

The look she gave him said louder than

words that she wasn't fooled. "If you don't want to give me a straight answer, I can take a hint."

"Fine." He waved his hand in dismissal before she could probe deeper into his motives — motives he didn't understand himself. He picked up the phone and, with renewed determination, launched into his plea for the loan of an ambulance.

When he finished his call, he had the satisfaction of knowing the company was at least considering his proposal. He had begun putting away his papers and shutting down his computer when Jennifer came in and held out a thick manila folder.

He scowled at her. "What's this?"

"The map you asked for and the file on the Shetland pony you did hip surgery on last spring. Remember fat Dolly? The family was from Medicine Falls. I thought since you were going out that way, you could do a follow-up visit to see how they're getting along. Besides, it's a better excuse than saying you thought you'd take a drive. The whole, 'I just happened to be in the neighborhood' line is kind of lame, but this way you can back up your story with a straight face."

"I don't need an excuse to go for a drive. This is a free country."

"I believe Sergeant Mandel will agree with you when you see her in Medicine Falls. Did you know they're putting on a performance tomorrow?"

"And how do you know that?" Had she been eavesdropping on his conversation with Lindsey?

"Avery told me. He drove Lindsey out here this morning. Isn't his accent the cutest thing?"

"I hadn't noticed."

She smiled. "Don't lose that map."

Brian opened his mouth to tell her he had changed his mind about going, but instead found himself saying, "Jennifer, I'm beginning to see you in a whole new light."

"Finally. I've worked here, what, two years? And this is the first time you've noticed that I'm a genius?"

"I was going to say I've begun to notice that you're rather devious."

"Oh. Well — only when I know it will help."

"Will help what?"

With a long-suffering sigh, she said, "Never mind. You'll figure it out.

Lindsey watched from the running board of the unit's candy-apple-red pickup as eight other members of her unit led their horses out of the matching red trailer emblazoned with the unit's name. The CGMCG was preparing for their last event of the season. The busy schedule of travel and performances over a five-state area would begin again in late spring. Usually by this time all the horses and riders were looking forward to a much-needed rest, but this year rest wouldn't be on the duty roster until after the trip to Washington, D.C., in late January.

All the men were looking forward to participating in the Inaugural parade with excitement and pride. The talk of late had been about little else.

Looking up, Lindsey noticed that the flawless blue sky overhead promised beautiful weather for the little town's special day. Even the relentless Kansas wind seemed to be taking a break. The flag jutting out from the ornately carved limestone post office hung quietly with barely a whisper of a breeze to ripple the Stars and Stripes. The stark branches of the trees that lined the streets radiating out from the town square were the only sign that fall had descended. The sun on Lindsey's shoulders was hot enough to make her glad she was wearing the unit's red T-shirt and not one of the dark wool uniforms.

"Lindsey!" Avery called from the rear of the truck where he was throwing a saddle on a gray gelding named Tiger. "My saber is in the back of the trailer. Can you get it for me?"

"Sure thing." She stood and moved toward the trailer, taking the time to speak softly so that all the horses knew she was passing behind them. In the trailer, she opened the door of the storage compartment and pulled out Avery's sword.

"Is that real?" a small voice asked behind her.

She turned to smile at two young boys who were obviously brothers. They boasted the exact same shade of ash-blond hair and identical pairs of bright blue eyes. The oldest boy looked to be about ten years old. She pegged the younger one at six or seven.

"Yes, this is a real saber. It's a replica of the type used by the U.S. Cavalry back in the Civil War. If your parents take you over to the rodeo arena after the parade, you can see how they are used."

"Wow," said the littlest, wide-eyed youngster.

"Told you it was real," his brother said smugly.

"But soldiers don't ride horses anymore. They drive jeeps and tanks," the younger one stated with a glare at his older sibling.

Lindsey vividly remembered arguing with Danny over silly things when they were kids. Her memories of him were good ones, she realized. For the first time since his injury, those memories didn't bring pain, but rather a quiet joy.

"You're right," she said. "Modern soldiers do drive jeeps and tanks, but there are special units like mine that are keeping the traditions of the Old West cavalry alive. We are real soldiers and this is our job."

"Cool."

"Way cool. Can I hold the sword?"

She shook her head. "I'm afraid not."

Clearly disappointed, the young pair took off back into the crowd forming along one side of the town's main street.

Lindsey carried the saber to Avery. He tipped his head in the direction to the boys. "New recruits?"

"Maybe. The little one would have been more impressed if you had a tank instead of a horse."

"Boys and their toys."

"You know that's true," Lee Gillis said as he led his horse over to stand beside them. "How's the arm, Lindsey?"

"Not painful as long as I don't bump it, but I still can't feel my fingers or use my hand. I won't be riding for a while. Who gets to stay behind with me?" Lindsey asked, looking over the line of saddled horses.

"Captain said to leave Socks with you. He's been a little nervous since the fall and we don't want him acting up in the parade. The Captain is riding Tiger."

"That's fine. Tiger will be happy he doesn't have to wait here while the rest of the boys run off and have fun."

Having one of the horses waiting beside the trailer was a good way to get people to stop and visit. Tiger, as the oldest and most calm four-legged member of the unit, usually had that honor.

Lee frowned as he looked toward the gray gelding standing alert at the end of the picket line. "I heard Captain Watson telling someone that it was time to retire Tiger."

If that was true, Lindsey was happy Tiger would be able to participate today. "He's been with the unit for more than fifteen years. That's a long time."

"What will happen to him?" Lee asked.

Shane patted his shoulder. "Don't worry. We'll find a good home for him."

Once the unit was mounted and ready to proceed, the grand marshal, who was also the mayor and the local grocery-store owner, fired a starter pistol into the air and the small-town parade began. The floats might have been put together on hay wagons, but they had been decorated with as much care and pride as any Rose Bowl entry.

All along the street people rose from lawn chairs and curbsides to stand as the unit rode past with the flag unfurled and the horses' hooves clattering in unison. Farmers, mill workers and townsfolk alike took off their hats. Most placed a hand over their heart and, beside them, their children did the same. Here and there in the crowd, a few men saluted and Lindsey knew with certainty that those proud few knew exactly what price freedom asked.

As the parade moved away, Lindsey waited beside the pickup prepared to answer questions from people who were interested in military history, who were horse lovers, or who were simply curious about the unit. It was a part of her job that she truly enjoyed. Once the last float left the staging area, she didn't have to wait long before a few people began to gather around and venture close enough to pose inquiries.

It always touched and humbled her when people came up just to say they were proud of America's military or to say thank you for serving their country.

Lindsey had just finished telling several high-school-aged girls about what it was like to serve in the army when she spied a familiar figure walking toward her. Her heart gave a funny little leap. "Dr. Cutter, what a surprise. What are you doing here?"

"I was in the neighborhood . . . what I mean is . . ."

Lindsey thought she detected a blush on his tanned cheeks.

He cleared his throat and began again. "I was doing a follow-up visit on one of my patients and I remembered that you mentioned your unit would be here today. I thought I would see firsthand what type of work your horses do. It will help me better evaluate when Dakota will be fit to return to duty. I had a glimpse of what you do the day you fell, but I'd like to see the whole thing minus the pileup."

"I'd be delighted to have you attend our exhibition. When the men return from the parade route, we'll travel over to the rodeo arena and set up there."

"Great, I'll see you later."

"I'll look for you."

Brian found the rodeo arena without difficulty. It wasn't long before the parade ended and those planning on attending the Little Britches rodeo began filling the seats. Sitting on the wooden planks of the grandstands, he watched for Lindsey. He spotted her along with the other unit members when they rode into the arena on the back of a flatbed truck loaded with rails and jump pillars. Dressed in red shirts and matching red ball caps, they went into action with military precision.

Lindsey was in charge of carefully measuring the distance between jumps and directing their setup down the middle of the course. As she was doing that, other men marked off and placed a series of upright poles along one side. Yet another soldier walked onto the field carrying a huge bunch of red, white and blue balloons. Soon they were divided up and secured to the jump pillars.

Once they were finished, the truck pulled out of the gates and Lindsey, breathless and bright eyed, joined Brian in the stands.

"Are you ready to be amazed and awed by fabulous feats of skill and daring?"

"I'm ready." The words were barely out of his mouth before rock music began blaring from the loudspeaker. The gates opened and eight horses and riders thundered in and circled the enclosure at a gallop. By the time they had made their second pass around the area, Brian was entranced.

Dressed in blue period uniforms and with banners waving, the detachment looked exactly like a piece of Western history come to life.

At a shouted command that he couldn't quite understand, the group came to a halt, head to tail. A second shout of orders had the horses wheeling into a single line. Like the sweep hand of his watch, they all turned in tight formation. The inside horse was actually prancing backward as they kept a straight line until a full circle had been made.

"Pretty good, huh?" Lindsey leaned forward and grinned at him.

"Very impressive."

"You ain't seen nothing yet."

She was right. The line broke apart and reformed into a column of twos, then charged down the course flying over each balloon decorated jump. At the end, they split apart and galloped back to the start where they formed into twos again.

A unit member on foot walked into the area. He carried a red-painted milk jug in one hand. Stopping near the center, he turned to face the mounted men and held up the jug in his hand.

Lindsey leaned toward Brian. "In the old days they used melons to practice this."

All the soldiers drew their sabers. Suddenly, the first horse exploded off the line and charged toward the man on foot. With precision that Brian couldn't believe, the rider impaled the jug off the man's hand and bore it aloft like a trophy until he reached the far end of the arena. Wheeling his horse around he held his saber and the jug out to his side and raced back. A second horse and rider charged down the field and speared the jug from the extended saber as they flew past each other. All eight riders repeated the maneuver, transferring the jug from sword to sword at a full gallop without a single miss.

Brian looked at the small woman seated beside him. "Can you do that?"

"Sure. Piece of cake."

"Now *that* is amazing."

"There are about seven historical mounted color guards in the United States military, but we are one of the few that train in combat techniques. Here, there is no distinction between women and men and the jobs we perform."

"Did you know that the equestrian sports are the only Olympic event in which men and women compete as equals?"

"I did. Do you know that we have our own cavalry competitions?"

He shook his head. "No, but after watching this, I'd like to see one."

"You'll have to wait until next September. I forgot to ask, how is your other patient doing?"

He looked momentarily perplexed. "My other patient?"

"The one you came here to see?"

"Oh, right, that patient. Dolly is getting along very well. Her owners say she is doing everything she was doing prior to surgery and more. That consists mainly of eating a lot and giving rides to their grandchildren when they visit on the weekends. I've advised them on a better diet for her and stressed the need for more exercise."

"Like having the grandkids over twice a week?"

"Three times a week would be better."

She laughed. "It was never hard to convince me to ride a pony when I was a kid. Hopefully, Dolly's family is the same way. Do you have any children?"

The smile that had been lurking in his eyes vanished. His face turned stone cold so quickly that Lindsey was taken aback.

"My wife and our unborn child died in a car accident several years ago."

His voice held the hard edge she had noticed the first time she had spoken to him. Back then, she had wondered if his leg was giving him pain. Now, she knew his suffering went much deeper than that.

She laid a hand on his arm. "I'm sorry for your loss."

He stood up. "Thank you. If you'll forgive me, I just remembered that I have to get back to the clinic."

Surprised, she said, "Aren't you going to stay for the rest of our performance?"

"Another time, perhaps. Good day, Sergeant Mandel." He made his way out of the grandstands, leaning heavily on his cane.

Lindsey watched him walk away and couldn't help but think that he looked like a very lonely man, even with the festive crowd milling around him.

CHAPTER SIX

"Do we have everything?" Karen pushed a cardboard box in on top of a stack already filling the front passenger's seat of the Jeep nearly to the roof. The backseat was equally loaded.

"If you don't, that's too bad," Shane said, holding open the door for her. "Nothing else will fit in here."

"There's still room for a few more things," Karen insisted. Dressed in faded jeans and a pink cable-knit sweater with her blond hair pulled back in a ponytail, she looked much younger than twenty-one.

"Only because I'm not sitting in the driver's seat yet. Once I'm in, we won't have room for a toothpick. I may have to eat a box or two of cookies just to reach the gearshift."

She thrust her hands on her hips. "Don't you dare eat anything unless you pay for it, soldier."

"Yes, ma'am," he replied with a good-natured grin.

Lindsey listened to the exchange with a little smile playing on the edge of her lips. It didn't require mind-reading skills to see that Shane had taken a liking to her little sister. She wasn't sure how Karen felt about him, but she hoped nothing serious was forming.

She knew she was getting ahead of herself. A few smiles and jokes didn't make a relationship. They'd only known each other for a few weeks.

Almost exactly the same amount of time that she had known Brian.

Giving herself a mental shake, she dismissed the idea that Karen was interested in Shane. Knowing Karen's dislike of the military, and after seeing what had happened to Danny, Lindsey was sure her sister wouldn't want to become involved with a serviceman. Perhaps she should mention as much to Shane. He was a friend and she didn't want his feelings hurt.

"Are you sure you know where to take this stuff?" Karen asked as she moved aside and let Shane shut the door.

He didn't exactly roll his eyes, but he came close. "The east entrance of the K-State football field."

"Good. We'll meet you there. Lindsey, are

113

you ready to go?"

"I am. Thanks for doing this, Shane."

"Anything to help, Lindsey. You know the whole unit is rooting for Dakota. The Captain said his second surgery went well yesterday."

"According to Dr. Cutter, he removed the pins and replaced the cast without any problems."

The curt postoperative report yesterday had been the longest amount of time Brian had spent in her company since that day at Medicine Falls. He was obviously a busy man with a heavy surgery schedule, lectures to prepare and students to teach. Each time Lindsey saw him he seemed to be heading somewhere else. All week she had wondered if he was deliberately avoiding her.

Shrugging off the hurt that idea caused, she glanced into the packed vehicle. "You'd better get going. We'll meet you there."

Once Shane pulled away from the curb, Karen's liveliness visibly deflated, causing Lindsey to take a closer look. Karen seemed pale and there were dark circles under her eyes that she had tried to disguise with makeup. Without a word, Karen climbed into her blue sedan. It was then that Lindsey remembered her cell phone was still sitting in the charger in the living room. "I'll be with you in one second, Karen."

She dashed into the apartment, snatched up the phone and raced back down the steps. As she hurried around the front of the car to the passenger's side, she saw that Karen was resting her forehead on her hands at the top of the steering wheel. Opening the door, Lindsey slid into the seat. "Are you okay?"

Looking up, she gave Lindsey a wane smile. "I have a headache, that's all. I guess I stayed up too late baking last night."

"You've been baking for three days non-stop. I told you we would have enough. Just look at how much food the people on post donated. You didn't have to try and do it all by yourself."

"I wanted to do my part."

"You've done more than your part. You've been my driver, my cook, my nurse and my constant companion for the past two weeks. Why don't you stay here and lie down? I can catch a ride with someone else."

"Don't be silly, I'll be fine."

Lindsey wanted to believe her, but an hour later she could see that Karen truly wasn't feeling well. Once the tables and home-baked goodies had been set up outside the stadium, Shane returned to base, leaving the two women to hopefully sell all of their baked goods to hungry college football fans.

The day couldn't have been much better for a football game or for a bake sale, Lindsey decided. The temperature wasn't bad as long as she stayed in the sunshine. The bright rays kept the breeze from feeling cold until one of the white clouds with a flat gray bottom blocked the sun as it drifted past. Then, it wasn't hard to imagine that Thanksgiving was less than a week away.

Before long, they were doing a brisk business, but Lindsey kept one eye on her little sister. When they had a break in customers, she insisted Karen sit down and put a cool cloth on her forehead.

"That feels good. I'm sorry to be a drag, Lindsey. I don't get these headaches often, but when I do, they really take it out of me."

"You should go home and rest."

"I can't leave you to sell all this by yourself. Besides, how would you get home?"

"I could drive her."

Lindsey looked up in surprise to see Brian standing with a loaf of homemade bread in his hand. He wore a long-sleeved, pale yellow shirt tucked into khaki chino pants. The perpetual frown was missing from his face as he smiled at her.

After the way he had been avoiding her,

she hadn't expected to see him today.

"How much for this bread?" he asked, holding out a loaf.

"Two dollars," Lindsey answered, willing her suddenly erratic pulse to calm down and her voice to sound casual. He shouldn't have this effect on her, but every time she laid eyes on him, it was the same.

"Are you sure you don't mind driving Lindsey home, Dr. Cutter?"

"Please call me Brian. Of course I don't mind giving her a lift." He handed over the bills.

"But it's out of your way," Lindsey protested as she took his money. She wasn't prepared to deal with the emotions his sudden appearance evoked. She needed more distance between them, not less.

"I don't mind."

"Good, it's settled then," Karen cut in quickly. "You're an answer to my prayers."

If Lindsey didn't know better, she might have suspected that Karen was doing a little matchmaking. But because she knew her sister really wasn't feeling well, she swallowed any further protests.

"Go home and lie down, Karen. I can handle the sales by myself."

"You won't be by yourself. I can stay and help."

Brian's offer caught her off guard. "That's all right, I can manage."

"I'm sure you can, but I'm going to help anyway." He came around to her side of the table. With him close beside her, she noticed the crisp, spicy scent of his aftershave. All her senses suddenly seemed heightened. He began rolling up his sleeves and she took note of the tanned muscles on his forearms. His fingers were long and well manicured. He had the gentle but strong hands of a surgeon.

She looked up to find him watching her in return. Sunlight glinted off his blond hair. He didn't look the least bit grumpy. *Handsome* was the word that came to mind. Her breath caught in her throat. He definitely was good-looking when he wasn't scowling. So why did he want to spend time with her?

The flattering notion that he might enjoy her company as much as she enjoyed his was quickly discarded. She wasn't looking for a man in her life, handsome or otherwise.

Once Karen had gathered up her belongings and left for her car, Lindsey turned to Brian. "You don't have to stay or give me a ride. I can call one of my friends on base and have them come get me."

"I don't mind helping. Besides, you're going to be overrun with customers in a few minutes."

"Why do you say that?"

"My secretary saw your flyer about this sale and suggested I have an announcement made during the game. A lot of these kids saw your fall and I'm sure they'll want to help."

"That was very kind of you."

"Don't give me too much credit. It was Jennifer's idea."

"I'll have to remember to thank her tomorrow."

"You can, but don't overdo it. The woman already has a high opinion of herself."

Before Lindsey could think of something else to talk about, his prediction came true. The football game ended and they were swamped with fans eager to buy cookies, cakes and brownies for a good cause. A few people even made donations without buying anything.

Brian sat at the cash box making change while Lindsey stayed busy answering questions about Dakota and visiting with the customers. Whenever he had a free moment, he spent it studying her. Having one arm in a sling didn't appear to hamper her as she boxed up the requested items. She was a true people person with a ready smile and an easy laugh that everyone around her responded to. It was no wonder he found her attractive.

For the first time he admitted the truth of those feelings, but that didn't change the fact that she wasn't for him. She deserved someone with a whole heart to give her. He wasn't a whole man in body or in soul.

Thrusting aside his somber thoughts, he resolved to keep a tight rein on his feelings. He would be foolish to allow something other than a professional relationship to start between them.

Before long, the last bag of chocolate fudge was bought and paid for and Lindsey dropped into a folding chair beside him.

"I can't believe we sold everything."

"Everything except these cookies." He pushed the plastic bag with a dozen dark brown oatmeal cookies toward her.

Lindsey opened the Ziploc top and offered him one. "Please accept this humble payment in return for your help today."

He took the cookie and bit into it. "I see why they didn't sell. They're kind of burnt."

"I know." She zipped the bag shut and tossed it into a box at her feet.

He indicated the bare tables. "What do we do with these?"

"They belong to the college. We just

rented them for the afternoon. They can stay here."

"Are you ready to leave then?"

"I guess I am. Hey, didn't you have a loaf of bread in your hand earlier?"

He checked around. "It must have been sold out from under me."

"I'm sorry."

"Don't worry about it."

"I'll have Sergeant Link's wife bake you another one."

"You didn't bake it yourself?"

A bark of laughter escaped from her before she pressed her hand to her lips. "I made those oatmeal cookies. Baking is not one of my strengths as you can plainly taste."

He grinned. She didn't seem the least bit embarrassed to confess her shortcomings. He admired that. "What is one of your strengths?"

Wrinkling her brow, she considered his question. "Adaptability. That's my strength. I lived in five states and four countries before I turned twenty. I'm not even sure how many schools I attended as a kid."

"That must have been hard."

"It might have been worse if I hadn't had Danny and Karen. Having Danny looking out for us made it easier to always be the new kids. That and the riding schools. No matter where Dad was stationed he always enrolled us in riding classes."

"Where is your brother now?"

A deep sadness settled over her features. "He lives in Washington, D.C., but I wish he lived closer. Danny was wounded in action last summer. He's a quadriplegic, now. He's finally at home, but he still requires around-the-clock nursing care."

"I'm sorry."

"Thank you."

"So, do you ever get tired of moving around?"

She tilted her head to the side. "No. Karen hated it when she was little, but Danny and I did okay. Maybe someday I'll find a place that will make me want to settle down, but for now the army is my home."

He rose and grasped his cane. "That must be my cue to return you to your post."

She rose, too, and finished stuffing several empty boxes in a nearby trash barrel. "Are you sure you don't mind?"

"Not at all. I'm parked over there." He pointed across the emptying parking lot to his white truck.

Lindsey fell into step beside him, adjusting to his slower pace without any sign of impatience. The silence lengthened between them, but he didn't find it uncomfortable. At his truck, he unlocked the vehicle with his remote key. She moved without hesitation to the passenger side, not waiting for him. He tried to hurry and open the door for her. She realized what he was doing when their hands closed over the handle at the same time.

The softness of her skin caught him by surprise. The bones of her hand felt delicate and dainty beneath his palm. A warmth stole over him that had nothing to do with the sunshine beating down on them.

She gave him a chiding look. "Oh, pu-leeze. I can get my own door."

At least she seemed unaware of the effect she had on him. He strove to keep his voice neutral. "Perhaps, but my mother raised me to be a gentleman."

"And my father raised me to be a grunt."

"A what?"

"That's slang for a foot soldier."

"It's not a very nice term."

"It's not always a nice job."

"In a test of wills, I'll match my mother against your father any day of the week. They don't make them any tougher than she is. Please allow me." He nodded toward the door.

Slowly, she pulled her hand out from

beneath his. "You win. This time."

"Duly noted." He pulled open the door and waited while she climbed in.

Lindsey watched Brian move around to the driver's side and took a few quick breaths to calm her racing heart. Never had the touch of a man's hand unnerved her the way Brian's touch did. The idea that she might be attracted to him was something she didn't want to contemplate. Falling for him was a sure road to heartbreak.

"Please, Lord. More heartache is the last thing I need," she whispered under her breath before Brian opened his door.

He stowed his cane on a rack in the rear window and started the ignition without a word. The silence that had seemed so comfortable only a few minutes before now seemed tense. They were only a few blocks from the stadium when his cell phone rang. He pulled it from his shirt pocket. Lindsey listened to the terse conversation with interest. After a few questions, he gave brisk instructions to the person on the other end of the line and then snapped his phone closed.

"I'm sorry, Lindsey, but I have to get back to the clinic. I have an emergency coming."

"Don't worry, I totally understand. I'll call a cab or get a friend to pick me up at the hospital."

"Are you sure?"

"Absolutely. It will give me a chance to spend a little time with Dakota."

He pulled onto a side street to turn around and in a few minutes they were heading back the way they had come. At the clinic, he hurried inside and met with several young men and one young woman. Lindsey knew they were the senior students on call for that day. As they walked toward the surgical suites, Lindsey found herself standing in the reception area where a young girl in a colorful Western costume sat with an older man dressed in jeans and boots. His cowboy hat rested on the chair beside him. The young girl was sniffling into a tissue. The man put his arm around her shaking shoulders and spoke to her softly. Lindsey couldn't hear what they were saying, but it was obvious that these were the people with the injured horse.

Pulling her cell phone from her back pocket, Lindsey punched in Shane's number. If he wasn't free to give her a ride, she'd try Avery next. Shane answered on the third ring. She could hear the sounds of laughter and cheering in the background. "It sounds like you're having a party."

"I'm watching a football game with some

of the guys. What's up?"

"I'm looking for someone to give me a ride back to base."

"I thought Karen was driving you."

"She had a nasty headache so I sent her home early. I thought I had a ride, but it fell through."

"Bummer." He groaned loudly. A chorus of groans from his friends was followed by one lone cheer.

"What was that about?" she asked.

"Lee's team just made the tying touchdown. If they make this extra point, they'll move ahead at the half."

"Are Avery and Lee both there?"

"Yup."

"All right, never mind. I'll find another way back."

"Are you sure? Wow! Did you see that block? That's the way we Texas boys play ball!"

"Thanks, Shane. Enjoy your game." She hung up without waiting for his reply. It was obvious she was going to have to take a cab.

She walked up to the reception desk and asked the young man seated there for the use of a phone book. He had just handed it to her when Brian came back into the room. His face looked grimmer than she had ever seen it.

He walked up to the tearful young girl and sat down beside her. Lindsey tried not to listen in, but she couldn't help overhearing his words.

"I'm sorry. There isn't anything we can do for Storm. He is suffering a lot of pain. The kindest thing we can do is to put him to sleep."

The young girl's heartfelt cry tore at Lindsey's heart. Tears of sympathy pricked her eyes.

Brian awkwardly patted the weeping girl's shoulder, then rose to his feet. "You can come and say goodbye first, if you like."

As the pair went down the hallway, Brian stopped beside Lindsey. "Is someone coming to pick you up?"

"I was just about to call a cab."

"If you don't mind waiting a few more minutes, I can take you. I won't be needed here, after all."

"I'm so sorry."

"Thanks. Why don't you wait in my office?"

"I think I'd rather visit with Dakota. Whenever you're ready. Don't hurry on my account."

"This is the one part of my job I hate." He turned away and followed Storm's grieving family.

Lindsey walked down the hall and out into the large room that housed Dakota's stall along with eight others. Opening the gate, she slipped in and circled his neck with her good arm. He swung his head around and nuzzled her side briefly before lowering his head and closing his eyes. Leaning against his warm coat, she breathed deeply, drawing solace from his familiar scent.

"Dear Lord, offer Your comfort to those people and to Brian at this sad time. Let them know that You will wash away every tear and heal every heart."

She wasn't sure how long she stood there before she heard Brian's voice behind her. "There's something about the smell of a horse that makes you think of hot summer days and shady rests under the spreading branches of a tall cottonwood tree."

"I love the feel of them," she said softly, not looking up. "They feel like living silk over powerful muscles."

With each breath Dakota took, she listened to air rushing and rattling in and out of his lungs. His heartbeat was like a muffled drum, steady and strong, and yet so vulnerable.

Brian stepped closer. As if he were reading her mind, he said, "They are so powerful. It's always a shock when we see one get hurt."

She turned her face to look at him without letting go of Dakota. "Is it over?"

Brian nodded. "He was a four-year-old quarter horse and according to his young owner, he had the makings of a barrel-racing champion. It was such a shame."

"What happened to him?"

Brian moved up beside her and began to stroke Dakota's face. "He suffered a fracture of the pastern much like this fellow's. We see a lot of breaks like that in horses who make quick turns and sliding stops."

"Why couldn't you do surgery on him?"

"He started out with a simple break, but by the time the family got him here, he had done so much damage to the leg trying to stand in the trailer that we couldn't do anything for him."

"I don't understand."

"There was irreparable damage done to the soft tissue and blood supply by the broken bone fragments. If he could have been brought to us in an equine ambulance, we might have been able to save him."

"Do you have one?"

"Not at present, but I haven't given up hope. For the most part, you'll only see them at big racetracks like Belmont Park or

129

Santa Anita. However, I'm trying to persuade the company that makes them to loan us one to have on display during our conference here on January twenty-first."

"I remember seeing one on television when that Kentucky Derby winner broke his leg."

"They're quite expensive. It seems that the board forgot to add the money for one to my budget," he joked.

"We could hold another bake sale. I would contribute more cookies."

"Another burnt offering?"

Delighted to see the ghost of a smile on his face, she grinned. "I don't always singe them. The oven in my apartment is fickle. Some days it gets hotter than others."

"I'm sure that is totally true."

"Speaking of hot things, Dakota feels warm to me."

"Now that you mention it, he does. I see that he hasn't eaten much today. There's still feed in his bucket."

"That's not like him. He's always ready to eat. Do you think he's sick?"

Dakota coughed deeply. Alarm raced through Lindsey's body and her gaze shot to Brian's face. He pulled his stethoscope from the pocket of his lab coat and moved to examine the animal. After listening to the horse's chest, he stepped back. The frown she hated seeing was etched between his brows.

"What is it? What's wrong?"

"I'll need an X-ray to confirm, but I'm afraid he's developed pneumonia."

"That's bad, isn't it?" She knew it was a stupid question the second the words were out of her mouth. Of course it was bad. Brian's look of deep concern only confirmed it.

CHAPTER SEVEN

Over the next days Dakota's life hung in a delicate balance. With his head held low he wheezed and coughed until Brian thought he couldn't possibly draw another ragged breath. It hurt just to watch him try. Brian knew minimizing the animal's distress was just as important as keeping him warm and well hydrated. Lindsey rarely left his side. Her presence seemed to bring the horse comfort. Somehow, her presence was a comfort to Brian, as well.

On the second night, a traffic accident with an overturned horse trailer brought in three more injured horses and the hospital's staff was stretched to the limit. With Brian's permission, Shane and Avery brought in a cot and placed it in an empty adjacent stall. All the unit members, Karen and numerous students took turns staying to help care for the animal. Their dedicated presence seemed to be all that was keeping the tired horse from slipping away.

Brian gave up going home and slept fitfully on the sofa in his office at night. During the daylight hours, the clinic operated normally and his surgery and teaching schedule kept him busy. At night, he rose every two hours to take vital signs and temperature readings looking for the least sign of improvement in Dakota. He could have left the horse's care to the senior students on duty, but he didn't. Dakota had become a special patient. Every four hours he gave the horse pain medication and every six hours he gave the massive doses of antibiotics needed to help stem the infection. In spite of all they were doing for him, Brian knew that it was Dakota's will to live that would ultimately be the deciding factor.

By the middle of the third night, he had given up urging Lindsey to rest. Instead, they worked side by side. While he administered the intravenous drugs, Lindsey held an inhaler over Dakota's nose to make sure he breathed in all the medicine designed to ease his labored respirations.

A few hours before dawn on the fourth night, Brian stifled a yawn as he leaned on the gate to Dakota's stall.

"You should go and rest," Lindsey suggested as she came to stand beside him.

"I'm all right, but I think your sister is out for the count." He nodded toward the cot in the next stall.

Lindsey looked over to see Karen had fallen asleep. "I can't say that I blame her. I feel like taking a nap myself."

"You're welcome to use the couch in my office."

"I may when I'm sure Dakota is doing better. What is his temperature now?"

Brian entered the stall and took a quick reading. "A hundred and five down from one hundred and six point five. His fever looks like it's breaking."

"Still, it isn't normal."

"No, it's not a hundred and one, but it's a definite improvement."

"Thanks to you." She entered the stall and held out a slice of apple. She was happy to see Dakota nibble it up.

"You're the one who has managed to coax him to eat. Nutrition is really important when a horse runs a fever." He gave a weary sigh as he sank onto a bale of straw in the corner.

"He's just used to me, that's all. Besides, apples are his favorite treat."

"I've noticed you slipping in horse chow and vitamins along with those slices."

"Do you think he is out of the woods?" She came over and sat on the bale beside him.

"In my professional opinion, I think he is."

"Are you ever wrong?" she asked.

"Frequently when it comes to people, but rarely about horses."

She managed a tired smile. "Are you saying you lack people skills?"

He called up a smile to match hers. "Why do you think I'm a vet?"

"You have been a blessing for us, that's for sure. I hate to think of Danny facing Dakota's loss on top of everything else he has been through."

Brian heard the catch in her voice and saw such pain on her face that he hesitated to ask any more questions. As if sensing his scrutiny, she glanced up and gave him a sad, sweet smile.

He reached out and covered her hand with his own. "Do you want to talk about it?"

"Danny was wounded while serving in Afghanistan. He singled-handedly saved the lives of two men in his unit when they were ambushed in a roadside attack. He risked heavy fire to pull those men to safety. Then, when a mortar exploded nearby, a piece of shrapnel hit him in the back of the neck and severed his spine."

"He sounds like a very brave man."

She looked toward the ceiling. "He is very brave. He's facing his disability with a determination that's amazing."

"It's all about having the will to live."

She studied him for a moment and then asked, "What happened to your wife?"

The question caught him off guard. He had never told anyone the details of the accident. For years he had kept those terrible hours and days locked away in his mind. He met Lindsey's gaze and saw only compassion looking back at him.

Sitting beside her in the dim building, he discovered a need to share his pain and his loss. "I had been working a lot of long hours that winter. I had only been out of school a year and I was intent on building up my practice. The Sunday before Valentine's Day, Emily planned to go visit her family. She wanted to share the news about the baby in person. I should have let her go alone. I was dead tired. If only I had let her drive . . ." His voice trailed off into silence.

"What happened?"

"While we were visiting her parents, the weather started to turn bad. She wanted to spend the night, but I wanted to get back. I thought my practice couldn't do without me for another day. I insisted we leave." He grew silent as the memory of the terrible night fanned the guilt he always carried.

"You don't have to tell me about it if you don't want to."

"I don't remember much about the accident itself. I do remember how hard it was to keep my eyes open looking into the snow. I must have fallen asleep at the wheel."

He patted his leg. "When I woke up rescue workers were cutting me out of what was left of our car. I reached for Emily. I found her hand in the darkness and then I felt her leave me. I felt her spirit touch mine and then she was gone."

"I'm so sorry."

Instead of answering, Brian rose and took another temperature reading on his patient. He had exposed enough of his soul for one night. "The fever is definitely going down."

"Thank the Lord for answering our prayers."

"I would say it is thanks to modern medicine."

"Perhaps the Lord's plan called for both medicine and prayers."

"I doubt it. I'm sorry. It's just that I gave up praying a long time ago."

"Because of Emily?"

He wanted to say yes, but he wasn't sure the words would make it past the lump in his throat.

She laid a hand on his arm. "It's okay. God will be there when you are ready to pray again."

"I don't think much of a God who allows terrible things to happen to good people."

"The Lord never promised that we wouldn't suffer. He did promise that He will always be with us."

"You surprise me."

"Why?"

"Religion and a military life don't seem to go together."

She smiled slightly. "Maybe not to you, but to most of us serving our country, it makes perfect sense. If I'm called to put my life on the line, I know that God has my back."

"Didn't your brother's injury leave you with doubts about that?"

"My brother's injury left me with the same anger and grief that everyone feels at a time like that. What God gives me is comfort, and the sure and certain knowledge that He is with me. My strength comes from Him."

Deciding it was time to change the subject, he asked, "Whatever possessed a woman like you to enlist in the army in the first place?"

She looked at him askew. "Why shouldn't a woman join the army?"

"I not saying a woman can't do the job. I'm just wondering why a woman would want to. You could be sent into a combat zone."

"You mean people might shoot at me?"

"Well, yes."

"Here's a news flash. I've been trained to shoot back. I even have a gun."

"Would you? Shoot back, I mean?"

"Yes. Does that make me a bad person in your eyes?"

"Of course not. Do you plan to make it a career?"

Leaning against the wall, she stretched her legs out and stared at her feet. "You have to understand that I come from a military family. The Mandels have served with distinction since the Civil War. Growing up, I always knew that I would enlist when I was old enough. I don't think my father would have approved of any other choice. He certainly wasn't happy when Karen started talking about becoming a teacher instead of a soldier."

"Teaching is an admirable profession."

"Not for a Mandel."

"So will Karen enlist, too?"

"Not for all the tea in China. She has stated categorically that she has no interest in wearing fatigues or taking orders from strangers."

"What does your mother think about your career choice?"

It was the first time Brian had seen uncertainty and regret in her eyes. She looked down and plucked a piece of straw from the bale. "My mother doesn't care one way or the other."

Brian sat down beside her. "What makes you say that?"

Fighting back ugly memories, Lindsey wrapped the piece of straw around her finger like a wedding ring. When she realized what she was doing, she pulled it off and threw it aside. "My mother left my father when I was ten. Two days before my birthday, actually. We never heard from her again."

"That must have been rough," he said gently.

"We managed." Only because she, Danny and Karen had had each other. Their father had retreated into his work, the work their mother had hated. He spent long hours away from home, and it wasn't long before he was transferred to a new post. After that,

Lindsey gave up watching for her mother to come back.

It was at the new base that they met a wonderful man by the name of Chaplain Carson. A kind and generous man, he always made time for the lonely kids who lived next door. In more ways than one, he helped all of them through that terrible time as he taught them about God's love.

"Does your father still feel the same way about the service after your brother was wounded?"

Brian's question jerked Lindsey out of the past. "I'm sure my father suffers as any man must suffer to see his son injured and hurting. But Dad is as proud as I am of what Danny did."

"Of course. I just thought that he might want you out of harm's way."

"He worries, but he knows I'll do my duty. It's up to me to carry on the family tradition. My father doesn't have to tell me that. It's understood."

"What would you do if there wasn't an army?"

She scowled at him. "What kind of question is that? There will always be an army. 'The price of freedom is eternal vigilance.' Thomas Jefferson said that and he was right."

"But what if you couldn't stay in the service for some reason? What would you do?"

The question was so foreign that Lindsey wasn't sure how to answer it. It had always been the army or nothing.

"Come on," he coaxed. "Think outside the box."

"I honestly don't know."

"What did your father do after he retired?"

"Drove us nuts."

Brian chuckled and Lindsey found to her surprise that she adored the sound. Still, she wanted to change the subject, so she asked, "What do your parents do?"

"They're ranchers. My family owns a spread outside of Missoula, Montana. They both still work as hard as they ever did, according to my older brother. He ranches with them."

"Why didn't you stay in the family business?"

"That's a long story."

She glanced at her watch. "Looks like I have time to listen."

"Okay. Long story short. As a kid, I was reckless. I thought more about impressing my friends than my own safety. One day, on a dare, I tried to ride my horse down the side of a steep embankment the way they do in the movies. We fell. How I wasn't killed outright I'll never know, but my mare broke both her front legs. When my friends brought my father to the scene, Dad gave me the rifle and told me to put her down because it was obvious her life didn't mean anything to me."

"What a cruel thing to say."

"Maybe it was, but he was right."

"Did you do it?"

"I couldn't, so my father did. But that day I vowed I'd never be the cause of another horse's suffering. I knew then that I'd be a vet."

"And you never wanted to be anything else?"

"Occasionally, I have this recurring desire to work in a movie theater and make popcorn."

"You're kidding, right?" She stared at him in amazement.

"Think about it. The smell of buttery popcorn all day long. Can't you just imagine it?"

Lindsey closed her eyes. "The sound of the popper and the sight of fluffy white kernels pouring out from under a silver lid."

"Can you think of a better job?"

"Driving a tank," she stated without hesitation. "You'd never be caught in another traffic jam. You could roll over anything in your way."

"Parking on campus might be a problem, though."

"Not a bit. Find the space you want and park on top of the car that's there." She glanced at him trying to control the laughter building inside. "After all, who is going to argue with a woman in a tank?"

"Good point. Can I rent one from you?"

She giggled and he began to laugh outright. His laugh had a wonderful, deep timbre. One she wanted to hear over and over again.

His smile slowly faded. "Since it looks like Dakota is through the worst of it, I'd better get home for a few hours and make up with Isabella."

The name was like a douse of cold water on Lindsey's joy. Did he have another woman in his life? The thought was a sobering one. Then the realization hit her. It mattered. It mattered more than she cared to admit. She swallowed hard. "Who is Isabella?"

"My bunny."

She wasn't quite sure she'd heard him correctly. "Your bunny. As in rabbit?"

He looked at her sharply. "Yes. Why is that so odd?"

She grinned, almost giddy with relief. "I'm not sure. I guess I pictured you as the kind of guy who kept a bulldog or maybe a python."

"Sorry to disappoint you. All I have is a domineering French Lop."

"I sense a story."

He glanced at his watch. "One that will have to wait for another day. I'll be back in a few hours. I have a surgery scheduled for eight o'clock this morning. You have my beeper number if you need me. I only live about ten minutes away."

"Dakota seems much better. I'm sure we'll be fine on our own for a few hours."

"There is always a student on duty if you need anything. I'll see you later."

"Good night, Brian."

He stood and she rose to face him. The air between them suddenly seemed charged with electricity. She longed to reach out and smooth his rumpled shirt. She wanted to comb her fingers through his tousled hair and coax it into some kind of order. Instead, she stuffed her hand into the hip pocket of her jeans and took a step back.

For a long moment, he simply stared into her eyes, then with a nod, he walked away. It wasn't until then that she remembered to breathe.

A few hours later, Dakota's temperature had fallen to a normal level. His appetite returned with a vengeance and he made short work of any apple slices that came within range. When Lindsey turned away to pull another piece of fruit from the brown paper bag by the cot, he whinnied loudly, waking Karen.

She sat up rubbing her eyes. "That sounds like he's feeling better."

"Much better."

"What time is it? Or maybe I should ask what day is it?"

Lindsey glanced at her watch. "It's the day before Thanksgiving and it's after nine."

"Why did you let me sleep so long?"

"You looked so peaceful that I didn't have the heart to wake you."

Tipping her head first to the right and then to the left, Karen winced. "My neck would have been happier if you had. Where is Brian?"

"He had a surgery this morning."

"You two seemed to be getting along rather well last night."

"I thought you were asleep?"

"I was — most of the time. What did you and he find to talk about until the wee hours of the morning?"

"This and that. You know how it is. Small

talk mostly."

"Small talk?" Something in Karen's expression told Lindsey that she wasn't buying that line.

"All right, if you want me to admit that I'm beginning to like the guy, I will."

"I thought so." She folded her arms over her chest and looked smug.

Lindsey turned away and began to toss flakes of hay into Dakota's stall. "Just because I like him doesn't mean anything except that it will be easier to keep working with him."

"I wouldn't be too sure about that. I sense more than a casual interest."

"I'm not looking for love, Karen, if that's where this is going. I have plans to make the army my career. Marriage and the military don't mix. Not for me, anyway."

"You're thinking about Mother. Just because our parents couldn't make their marriage work isn't any reason to believe you can't make a relationship work. I don't remember much about Mom because I was only six when she left, but from all that Danny has told me, I can see you are a much stronger woman than she was. You have a good heart and a strong faith. Why not trust that God will bring the right man into your life?"

She glanced at Karen. "What makes you think Brian is the right man?"

Karen stepped up and took her by the shoulder. Giving her a gentle shake, she said, "Girlfriend, what makes you so sure he isn't?"

CHAPTER EIGHT

The Monday after the holiday weekend, Brian sat in his office trying to concentrate on drafting a letter of appeal for funds to buy an ambulance when he noticed Isabella creeping toward his Wildcat mug. He knew that look in her eye. Picking her up before she could snatch one of his freshly sharpened pencils and chew it into splinters, he scolded softly, "I see what you're trying to do. I've got to get this letter done, so that means you have to go outside."

Outside was one of her favorite words. She loved racing up and down the long fenced area he'd had built beside the building and nibbling on the fresh grass.

He needed a break anyway. The words on his yellow legal pad weren't anywhere near the tone he wanted to convey. Instead of fine-tuning his letter, all he had done that morning was think about Lindsey.

Rising, he picked up his cane from where

it leaned against his desk and made his way toward the door. As he pulled it open, Isabella suddenly leaped out of his arms and took off toward the stall area. He hurried after her, knowing she could easily be hurt if she ran into one of the occupied pens. Fortunately, he saw the double doors at the end of the hall were closed.

He was only a step away from his pet when one of the doors opened and two students came through. It was all the opportunity Isabella needed.

"Catch her," he called out.

By the time the befuddled students realized what he was talking about, the rabbit had darted between them and through the doorway.

"Isabella, come back here!" His shout did nothing to stem her headlong flight.

Running past the students, Brian entered the stall area and scanned the large enclosure for any sign of his fleeing pet. Checking each pen as he hurried past, he didn't see Private Barnes until he almost ran into him.

"Whoa, there, Doc. What's the rush?"

"Did you see a rabbit come this way?"

"A what?"

"Isabella is loose?" The familiar female voice made Brian looked past the young soldier. Jennifer was sitting on a folding chair beside the army cot, but she jumped to her feet, a look of alarm on her face.

Happy to have an ally who understood what was needed, Brian nodded. "Make sure all the outside doors are closed."

She grabbed the soldier's arm. "Of course. Avery, you go that way and I'll make sure everything on this end is shut. Give a shout if you see her."

"What sort of rabbit am I looking for?"

She rolled her eyes and gave him a shove. "The fuzzy kind that hops. Now hurry, but don't scare the horses."

Brian retraced his steps and began searching more slowly. There were numerous bales of hay and bags of feed stacked along the center of the wide aisles. She could be behind any of them or under the wooden pallets they rested on.

He'd only finished checking a small area when Jennifer returned. "None of the outside doors are open. I've left Avery in charge of seeing that no one goes in or out."

Brian stared around the large building. "Why would she suddenly decide she wanted to come in here? She loves going outside. I distinctly told her she was going outside."

"That may be my fault," Jennifer admitted with a pained look. "I brought her out here with me yesterday."

"And why were you out here instead of at the desk?"

"Avery . . . that is . . . Private Barnes asked for some help with the thermal thermometer."

His scowl prompted her to add quickly, "I held on to Isabella the whole time. I didn't let her run loose. She wasn't even frightened by the horse when he came over to check her out."

Brian sighed, trying to hide his vexation. "All right, we'll talk about this after we find her. You take that aisle and I'll take this one. Check everywhere."

"We don't have to. There she is."

He turned to see Jennifer pointing toward Dakota's stall. The big horse was lying down with his legs tucked under him. His neck was arched as he sniffed the bunny cuddled up against his chest. Brian approached the stall slowly. He didn't want to startle Dakota into lunging to his feet. One misstep and the little rabbit could be seriously injured, or worse.

"Come here, Isabella," he called softly. Dakota looked up at the sound of his voice, but the rabbit didn't move. Brian didn't see any choice. He would have to go in and get her.

"All right, big fella, you just stay relaxed." Brian opened the gate slowly and stepped inside the stall. Dakota threw his head up as if he was about to rise.

"Stay down, Dakota." The command came from behind Brian. He shot a quick look over his shoulder. Lindsey stood at the gate.

"He'll stay still now. It's okay," she assured him.

"How can you be so certain?"

"It's what he's been trained to do. He has to follow orders just like the rest of us."

Trusting her word, Brian walked to the pair and scooped up Isabella. She squirmed and tried to get down again, but he held on tightly.

Lindsey arrived beside them and squatted to pat Dakota's neck. "They look so cute together. Why don't you leave her here. She certainly seems to make him happy."

"It would be too risky." Brian ran his hand down Isabella's long, soft ears. "Lindsey, allow me to introduce you to Isabella the Terrible."

Rising, Lindsey stroked the rabbit's small round head. "You don't look very terrible to me."

"Reserve judgment until you know her better," Jennifer suggested. "Shall I take her outside?"

Brian shook his head. "No, I'll take her and then you and I are going to have a talk in my office."

"Yes, Doctor." She turned away meekly and left the building.

"I can't believe it," he said in astonishment.

"What?"

"She always has some sort of snappy comeback."

"Maybe she's saving it until you're alone."

"That's a scary thought." He made a mental note to be gentle with his secretary when he took her to task for neglecting her duties.

He glanced at the woman beside him.

Thoughts of Lindsey kept him from sleeping, kept him from working, and, worst of all, they kept him from thinking about Emily. It certainly wasn't Lindsey's fault, but he had decided it would be best if he didn't see as much of her in the future. During the past two days, he had accomplished his goal with difficulty. Like today, she always seemed to turn up when he least expected her.

Determined to put some distance between

them now, he said curtly, "I have to put Isabella away. Excuse me."

Lindsey watched his abrupt retreat and wondered why he always seemed to be rushing out the door as she came in. After their exchange of confidences during Dakota's illness, she felt she had gained a better understanding of the man, perhaps even made a friend. Obviously, she had been mistaken. Brian couldn't have made it plainer that he didn't need or want her friendship.

"Not a very sociable chap, is he?" Avery said, coming to stand beside her.

She felt compelled to defend Brian in spite of his recent attitude. "He can be."

"I'll take your word for it."

"Where have you been?"

"Jenny had me guarding the doors to keep the rabbit from getting away. She stopped by to tell me the rodent has been recovered. Where was she?"

"Making nice with Dakota."

"No joke? I didn't know horses and rabbits got along."

"I've seen horses that weren't happy unless they had a stall mate. Usually it's a pony, but I've seen them adopt goats or dogs, so why not a rabbit?" Lindsey said.

"If it helps Dakota get better, I'll buy him a whole herd of rabbits."

"I'll second that. Speaking of Dakota, how is he today?"

"Relaxed, eating and drinking well. I'd say he's much improved. And how are you? You saw the doctor again today, didn't you?"

"The bone is mending, but I still don't have feeling in my fingers or my hand."

"How much longer does he think that will last?"

"You know doctors. It could be a week, it could be a month. Time will tell."

"Bummer."

"No kidding. It sure would be nice to be able to drive myself again and not have to depend on everyone to get me places. Karen is a doll, but I think even she is tired of being my chauffeur."

"Is your car a stick?"

"No, why?"

"Because if it isn't a stick, then you only need one arm to drive. Get a spinner for your steering wheel."

"What's that?"

"A kind of doorknob that attaches to the wheel and allows you to steer with one hand."

"Isn't that only for handicapped people?"

"Have you looked in the mirror? You *are*

handicapped even if it's temporary. But no, they aren't only for the people with disabilities. I've got one on my sports car."

"Don't tell me, let me guess. So you can keep one arm around a girl while you're driving your Jag?"

"Exactly."

"How did a guy like you end up in the army?"

"You mean how did one of Boston's most eligible bachelors find himself enlisted as a private?"

"Yes. I've been wondering about that."

"So have I. My grandfather has some explaining to do when I get home. And for the record, the evils of alcohol can not be overstated."

"You got drunk and ended up enlisted?"

"I'm ashamed to admit that I was so plastered I don't remember, but even my grandfather's lawyer couldn't get me out of Uncle Sam's contract. If he actually tried."

"Why wouldn't he?"

"I've done a lot of dumb things in my life. I was careless and selfish because I thought money fixed everything. My grandfather was at his wit's end with me. Maybe he thought the army could straighten me out."

"I think he was right."

A half smile pulled at one corner of his

mouth. "It's nice of you to say so. At least I've given up drinking anything stronger than soda."

Lindsey patted his shoulder. "The Lord moves in mysterious ways."

"So does my grandfather," he grumbled.

"The spinner is a good idea. Would you be able to put one on my car if I gave you the money to buy one?"

"It would be my pleasure. But before you get behind the wheel, I insist you let me take you to an empty parking lot for some practice before you try it alone."

"You've got a deal. Thanks, Avery. Now, you're relieved. Is there anything I need to know about Dakota?"

"The Doc wants us to keep checking the cast for hot spots with the thermal thermometer at least once every four hours."

"Any signs of pressure sores?"

"No, his leg is as cool as a cucumber, but he is getting up and down more and that could cause problems. Are you taking leave for Christmas?"

"I hadn't planned on it. I don't want to desert Dakota after his close call." Voicing her excuse out loud didn't lessen the nagging guilt she had been saddled with since her conversation with Karen that morning.

"What about your family?"

"Karen has decided to spend the holidays with my brother since I won't be going home."

She dreaded the coming holidays. It was hard to think about celebrating Christmas with Danny's injury looming like a dark cloud over everyone's mood. "What about you?"

"I'll be here. Maybe we should have our own Christmas party."

"That's a good idea. I'll talk to the Captain about it."

After Avery left, Lindsey walked into the stall and sat down beside Dakota. He nuzzled her shoulder briefly, then began nipping at her pocket.

"Okay, I do have a few alfalfa treats in there, but don't get greedy. You're not the only horse in this place. See that little pinto across the way?" She pointed to a pony across the aisle. Dakota ignored her extended arm.

"He likes alfalfa, too, so you'll have to share." She pulled a handful of green pellets from her pocket and held them out for him. He lipped them up quickly.

After visiting with the horse for half an hour, Lindsey rose and began walking between the pens, stopping to visit with several other inmates. At the end of the building she glanced out the window and saw Isabella racing back and forth in a wire run.

Slipping out the door, Lindsey stopped beside the rabbit's kennel and knelt down to put her fingers through the chain links. Isabella stopped running long enough to investigate the potential new playmate. "Have you been banished from his office?"

She glanced toward the front of the building. "Care to share any secrets about your owner? Do you know why he's treating me like a plague victim?"

Isabella sniffed at Lindsey's fingers then dashed away. "I can see you aren't going to be any help."

From inside the barn, Lindsey heard Dakota's whinny. Rising, she headed back into the building. With only horses and rabbits to talk to, it promised to be a long day. Mainly because the one creature she really wished to spend time with had retreated to his office and she couldn't think of a good reason to follow him.

It was late afternoon and Lindsey had just closed the book she was reading when the sound of raised voices reached her.

Brian stormed through the doorway. A deep frown etched a groove between his eyebrows.

Jennifer was hard on his heels. "I didn't take her out of her pen, honest."

"Is she in here?" he demanded, stopping in front of Lindsey.

Not a word all day and now he had the nerve to behave like this? He wasn't the only one capable of pretending indifference. "More rabbit troubles, Doctor?" she drawled.

"Isabella has never run away before. You want me to believe she's done it twice in one day?"

"Dakota and I haven't seen hide nor hair of her, have we, boy? How much trouble is it to keep track of one bunny?" She rose from the cot where she was sitting and looked toward her horse. He stood in the corner of his pen with his head down. She assumed he had been sleeping. It was then she noticed the small bundle of fur beneath his nose.

Brian spotted his pet at the same time. "She *is* here."

Taken aback, Lindsey turned to him. "I'm sorry. I never saw her come in. I was outside by her pen for a little while, but I didn't take her out. She was inside her run when I left."

"I seriously doubt a six-pound rabbit could open a kennel door and then a barn door all by herself."

"I wouldn't put it past her," Jennifer muttered.

Brian glared at her but didn't allow himself to be diverted. "It isn't safe to let her in with Dakota no matter how cute you think it is."

Lindsey opened her mouth and closed it again. Anger at his accusation momentarily robbed her of speech. She took a step toward him.

"Are you saying you think I took your precious rabbit out of her cage and put her in with my lame horse just because I thought they looked cute together?" Resentment lent a steely edge to her words.

"You go, girl." Jennifer crossed her arms and looked smug.

Brian took a step back. Lindsey could see the indecision wavering in his eyes. "If this is another one of your harebrained ideas for stress reduction . . ."

"I have no idea how your rodent found her way out of her pen and into here, but I had nothing to do with it."

"Rabbits aren't rodents, they're lagomorphs," Jennifer supplied with a bright smile.

"My horse doesn't need a lop-eared fur ball to reduce his stress and keep him company. He has me. Perhaps if you paid more attention to *your* pet, she wouldn't be looking for love in all the wrong places."

"Lagomorphs have four upper incisors. The second pair is peglike and posterior to the first. Rodents only have two upper incisors."

Both Lindsey and Brian turned to stare at Jennifer.

"Well, it's true. A rabbit *isn't* a rodent. I can't believe the pair of you. There's absolutely nothing wrong with a hare's brain and don't ever say *rodent* like it's a bad word."

Brushing between Brian and Lindsey, Jennifer slipped through the gate into the stall and picked up Isabella. Slipping out again, she paused and looked from Brian to Lindsey and back. "Any more name-calling and someone is going to find their mouth washed out with soap. Apologies are in order, and I mean now."

Lindsey watched Brian's secretary exit through the main doors with the squirming rabbit under her arm. Dakota whinnied frantically as his new friend was carried away.

Without taking her eyes off the doorway, Lindsey asked, "Did she mean it?"

He stood beside her looking in the same direction. "I'm not sure, but I'm not taking any chances. I'm sorry I suggested you were harebrained."

"I've been told there's nothing wrong with a hare's brain, so apology accepted. I'm sorry I called Isabella a rodent."

"You're forgiven."

"She's kind of a weird woman," Lindsey ventured.

"I had no idea until recently just how strange she is," he acknowledged.

Glancing at Brian from the corner of her eye, Lindsey suddenly found herself overcome with giggles. Brian shot her a dour look but couldn't keep the smile off his face. A second later he was chuckling, too.

By the middle of the following week, Dakota's condition had improved enough to allow him to be transferred back to the base stables. With the unit members providing around-the-clock care, Brian knew there wasn't any reason to keep the horse at the clinic. Except that it meant he wouldn't be seeing Lindsey anymore.

The day after the big bay left it suddenly became a much quieter building. At least twice before noon Brian found himself standing beside the empty stall and staring into the space. He should be wondering how Dakota was getting along, but he had confidence that Lindsey and the men would follow his instructions to the letter. What he found himself wondering was how Lindsey was getting along. What was she doing? Was she resting her arm the way she should, or would she be trying to do too much?

Jennifer came up beside Brian and propped her chin on the rail. "I miss him already."

"He'll get the best care possible and he'll be happier in his own stall with the other horses he knows."

She sighed. "I know the horse will be happier, but I'm not sure the rest of us will be."

Puzzled at her depressed tone, he looked at her closely. "You're not taking about missing the horse, are you?"

"Duh? I'm talking about that gorgeous hunk."

"Forgive me if I seem a little slow, but which hunk would that be?"

"Private Avery Barnes. That Boston accent of his was to die for. Can't you think of some reason to send me out to the base?"

"Jennifer, if Private Barnes is interested in seeing you again, he'll call."

"Oh, like you're going to call Lindsey?"

"That's neither here nor there."

"Which means, no." She shook her head as she walked away muttering, "Men are *so* not bright."

At the doorway, she stopped and looked back. "How is it that so many of you are in charge of stuff?"

Brian watched her walk out without replying. He had no intention of seeing Lindsey unless it was in an official capacity. He liked her, but it would never be more than that. The love of his life was dead and he knew there would never be another.

Yet, he did miss Lindsey.

He rested his arms atop the cool metal bar of the gate. The hay bale where they had shared bits and pieces of their lives still sat in the corner of the stall. In those hectic hours when Dakota had been so ill, Brian had learned a lot about Lindsey Mandel.

She was dedicated and tireless when it came to doing her duty. She was witty and funny, often when he least expected it. The mental image of her parking a tank outside the clinic made him smile even now. She was sure of her place in the world and that place was in the army. Yet she didn't believe in mixing marriage with her career.

It was a shame, really. She had so much to offer. She was more than a pretty face. She was a woman with a heart and a soul. Her faith in God seemed unshakable in spite of being abandoned by her mother as a child and her brother's devastating injury. She would make some man a fine wife if he didn't mind her going off to war.

Like most Americans, he listened to news and saw almost daily the way brave young men and women sacrificed everything for the freedom he took so much for granted. He was ashamed to admit that he had thought of them as foolishly brave. But there was nothing foolish about Lindsey or about her love of country.

Emily would have liked her.

Pushing away from the gate, he made his way back to his office. He had a mound of paperwork waiting for him. The extra work would be good. It would help keep his mind off the void that had formed in his life. Lindsey and her horse were gone. Now his life could finally get back to normal.

But was that what he really wanted?

CHAPTER NINE

Lindsey ran the flat brush from Dakota's withers to his rump and worked down his side until his coat held a high shine. Inside the cavernous limestone stable that had been built in 1889, she listened to the sounds of other horses being led out for their morning exercise. Their shod feet clattered noisily on the uneven cobblestone floor. The cool interior smelled of old wood, horses, hay and oiled leather. It was a scent she had come to love in the sixteen months that she had been assigned to the unit.

The repetitive motion of brushing Dakota didn't require much thought, leaving her mind free to wander. The place it chose to go was back to the Large Animal Clinic.

Had Isabella managed another escape only to find Dakota gone? What was Brian doing today, Lindsey wondered? Was he thinking about her?

"A penny for your thoughts?"

She turned to see Shane leaning on the lower half of the wooden stall door and looking bored now that their season was over.

"They aren't worth that much," she replied, picking up a mane and tail comb.

"Need some help?" he offered.

"Sure. Trying to comb a tail one-handed is harder than it looks."

"How's the arm doing?"

"It hurts, it itches, and the fact that I can't use my hand is driving me nuts — other than that, it's fine."

"At least you don't have to stand on it." He motioned to the cast on Dakota's leg.

"I know. Poor boy, I can't imagine being uncomfortable and not being able to tell anyone."

"He'll tell us, just not with words."

"He has been nipping at the wrap today."

"See what I mean?"

Lindsey ducked under Dakota's neck and began grooming his other side. Shane spoke softly and patted the big bay's rump before pulling his tail to one side to comb it.

Lindsey glanced at him and her hand stilled.

"What?" he asked when he noticed her staring.

"Danny and I were doing this very thing

the last time I saw him before he was wounded. It was only a few days before he shipped out. Neither one of us wanted to say goodbye, so we worked side by side grooming Dakota without saying a word. Danny loves this horse. I thought he was crazy to pay boarding fees and buy feed on an enlisted man's salary, but he vowed he would trailer Dakota to any post in the U.S., including Alaska, rather than sell him. I think he would have taken him overseas if he thought it was safe."

"Karen said the same thing."

It was just the opening she had been looking for to ask Shane about his feelings for Karen, yet was it really any of her business? Because she cared for both of them, she took the plunge. "Shane, about Karen —"

"Rest easy." He cut her off before she got any further. "Karen is a wonderful person and as sweet as they come, but there isn't anything between us."

"I only wanted to say that I wouldn't object if there were. I think you're a great guy."

"I think I am, too," he agreed loudly. "Feel free to fix me up with any of your friends. This down-home Texas boy will show 'em a good time."

"I beg to differ," Avery said from the

doorway. "If any of your friends want to be treated like a lady, they need to go out with a gentleman like myself, not a hayseed cowboy."

Lindsey chuckled at their good-natured teasing. "I want to keep my friends, so I won't let them go out with either of you."

Avery wrinkled his brow. "Ouch."

Shane looked at him. "Did she just insult us?"

"Yes, but she did it with a smile. It makes me wonder if I should show her our new toy?"

Glancing between the two of them, she pressed her lips together, then said, "Okay, I'll bite. What toy?"

Avery held up a small gray case the size of a camcorder. "Our new thermal-imagining recorder. This way we can keep an infrared eye on Dakota's leg and report any hot spots or inflammation in his other legs before they get serious."

She ducked under Dakota's neck and came over to examine the camera. "This is great. Did Brian send it over?"

Shane shook his head. "No, your boyfriend didn't splurge on this. This is army issue."

"He isn't my boyfriend. How does it work?"

"I'll show you." Avery flipped up the

screen, pointed the camera at Dakota and a multicolored image of a horse appeared.

"What do the colors mean?" Lindsey pointed to the screen.

"Blue is cool. The warmer an object is, the closer to red it appears on the screen. See how the floor and walls show up as blue. Dakota is warmer than the floor. He shows up as greens and yellows."

"Except for that spot on his cast," she pointed out.

Avery moved closer. "Yes, he has quite a bit of heat coming from the lower portion of his leg."

"Does that mean there's a problem?"

"It means I'm going to give your boyfriend a call and have him check it out."

"Stop it. I told you he isn't my boyfriend."

Avery closed the camera and winked at Shane. "Methinks the lady doth protest too much."

Brian finished rewrapping Dakota's new cast with a bright blue elastic webbing designed to help prevent the horse from chewing on it.

"That was a good call, Captain. If the rub had gotten much worse we could have had a real problem with a pressure sore."

"Private Barnes is the one who found it."

"Your men have done a good job of looking after this fella." Rising from the short three-legged stool he used when he was out in the field, Brian patted Dakota's shoulder.

"We want to see him well and back on active duty."

"I hope that happens, Captain." Putting his supplies back into his case, Brian tried to sound casual. "Where is Sergeant Mandel today? When Dakota was at the clinic she stuck to him like a burr."

"She had to report for physical therapy up at the hospital."

"Her arm isn't worse, is it?"

"No, but there is some concern about the damage to the nerve. It's too bad, really. She and Dakota were to carry the U.S. flag in the upcoming Inaugural parade.

"She mentioned that Dakota needed to be healed enough to walk three miles with a rider by January twentieth."

"Do you think he'll be able to do it?"

"Six weeks in a cast would leave four weeks for rehabilitation and strengthening. He might be ready by then, but it's a big if."

"This ride is very important to Lindsey."

"Keep doing what you're doing and he may improve enough to go. I'll have some of our students check back in a couple of days to see how he's doing."

The two men shook hands and Captain Watson walked back to his office. Brian began repacking his bag and supplies into the special compartments built into the bed of his truck. He had just closed and locked the tool chest when a dark blue sedan pulled up beside him. The door opened and Lindsey got out. It was as if the sun had come out from behind the clouds.

"Hi," she said as she walked up to him.

"Hi." He couldn't think of anything else to say. Oddly enough, she seemed at a loss for words, as well.

He gestured toward her car. "I didn't think you could drive."

"Avery suggested I get a spinner for my steering wheel. It works great, but I still overcorrect a little. How's Dakota?"

"Fitted with a new cast and doing fine." The silence lengthened again. He closed the truck door.

"So, how is Isabella getting along?" Lindsey asked quickly.

"She's good."

"Not making any more escapes?"

"Not a one."

"Glad to hear it."

"I guess I'd better be going."

"Oh, sure. I didn't mean to keep you."

She took a step back, uncertainty clouding her eyes.

"I'll be back the day after tomorrow to check on Dakota. Maybe I'll see you then?" He knew he should send some of his fourth-year students, but he found he wanted the excuse to come back and spend time with Lindsey.

"Great. I'll look for you." Her bright smile tugged at his heartstrings.

He climbed into his truck and drove away. Glancing in his side mirror, he saw her watching him from the edge of the roadway. Resisting the urge to turn around and go back was the hardest thing he had done in a long time.

A week later, Lindsey was leaning against Dakota's stall door when she heard halting footsteps on the cobblestones behind her. She knew who it was without turning around and her heart gave a happy leap. Brian had been out to check on Dakota twice during the past week, but at the last visit, he had pronounced Dakota well on the way to recovery. Since there wasn't any problem with the horse, had he come to see her?

"Good morning, Lindsey." The sound of Brian's voice sent a sparkle of happiness shooting through her veins. She turned to face him, hoping her delight didn't show. "Good morning, Brian."

"How's my patient doing?"

"Getting better every day."

"I'm glad to hear it."

He stopped close beside her, his arm just brushing hers. She didn't pull away as she realized how much she had missed his company and how right it felt to be with him. "What are you doing here?"

"I want to take a few X-rays to document the bone's healing progress."

Of course he hadn't come just to see her. Lindsey pushed aside the tiny disappointment she felt and resolved to be content with his company no matter why he had chosen to come. "Do you need any help?"

"I will if you aren't busy."

"I'm afraid I have a tour due any minute. I'll get one of the other men to help."

"I'm not in any rush. What sort of tour?"

"It's a group of schoolchildren from Topeka."

"Is that why you're dressed in your itchy-looking blues?"

She brushed at the shoulder of her short cavalry jacket with one hand, then tugged the hem down as she stood up straight. "How do I look? Notice anything different

176

about me?"

"Is this a trick question?"

"No, I got my cast off yesterday."

"I see that now. Good for you, but you still have the sling."

"I don't have much feeling in my hand or arm yet. This way it isn't dangling against my side."

"Nerves heal slowly. Give it some time. Even with the sling, I think you look very nineteenth century."

"That's the idea." She dusted the top of her knee-high black riding boots by rubbing them on the back of each pant leg.

At the sound of a vehicle, she looked toward the parking lot and saw a small yellow school bus pulling up. She settled her cap snuggly on her head. "Pardon me while I see to our visitors."

Lindsey was proud of the CGMCG and she especially enjoyed giving tours to the dozens of Scout troops, grade-school classes and veterans' groups that visited the post each year.

Brian asked, "Is there any reason I can't join the tour? I'd like to know more about your unit."

"I'd be delighted to have you, provided you help keep the kids in line. I've found that the boys especially tend to get rowdy when no one is looking."

She put on her best welcoming smile and walked outside. In the courtyard, she noticed a wheelchair lift being lowered to the ground at the back of the bus. A middle-aged man waved to her and instructed the group of ten-year-old boys next to the van to stop horsing around. The girls, standing off to one side, were giggling and whispering to one another.

"Good afternoon, and welcome to the Commanding General's Mounted Color Guard stables."

"Hey, you're a girl." The biggest boy in the group smirked. "Girls can't be in the army."

"Actually, women serve in many units in today's military. But during the period when this stable was built, women were not allowed to enlist."

"Didn't a few women serve in the Union Army during the Civil War?" Brian asked.

She shot him a grateful look. "That's correct. Both the Union and Confederate Armies had women who fought disguised as men. It goes to show that women can be good soldiers and as brave as men in battle. If you'll come this way, we'll start our tour with the barn."

She paused inside the large double doors

where a life-size model horse stood before a wall displaying photographs of cavalry horses in action.

"Please watch your step. These old cobblestones can be treacherous." She gestured toward the uneven floor.

"Wouldn't it be better for the horses to have these torn up or paved over," Brian suggested.

She wrinkled her nose. "Don't think we haven't asked. Unfortunately, this is a historical building and can't be altered. This is the last remaining original stable building. It was constructed of native limestone and timber in 1889. It originally housed sixty mounts. At one time it was converted into a pistol range before being returned to its original function when our unit was formed. Before we get started, I'd like to have each one of you sign our guest book."

One by one, the children signed their names in a ledger on a podium until only the boy in the wheelchair was left. Brian took the book and handed it down to the youngster. The boy shyly smiled his thanks.

"As you can see," Lindsey continued, "our model horse, Stick and Stone, carries everything a cavalry horse would have been equipped with in 1880s. The saddle is called a McClellen and has the unique feature of an open split down the center and a rawhide seat. Would anyone like to guess why?"

The boy in the wheelchair raised his hand. Lindsey pointed to him. "Yes?"

"It allowed air to circulate and help keep the horse's back from getting sore?"

"That's right."

"Brainiac," one of the group muttered.

"The only thing he knows about riding a horse is what he reads in a book," the big boy scoffed.

As Lindsey led the group down farther into the barn, Brian replaced the visitors log and waited while the boy in the wheelchair struggled to maneuver his chair down the wide aisle.

"Do you need a hand?" Brian offered when it was obvious that the boy's wheels weren't rolling well over the uneven stones. He put his hands on the handles of the chair.

"No, I can manage," the kid said defensively, pushing harder.

"I'm sure you can. I only offered because . . . please don't tell anyone . . . but walking on a rough surface like this makes me afraid of falling."

The child looked back at him. "It does?"

"Would you mind if I just held on to the back of your chair to steady myself?"

Sitting up straighter, the boy shrugged. "I guess that would be okay."

"We'd better catch up with the group or we'll miss the tour."

"I'm not really interested in it anyway."

"You don't like horses?"

"They're okay."

"Their big size can make them scary." Brian tipped the wheelchair backward slightly freeing the front wheels.

"I'm not scared of them."

"You're not? That's good. My name is Brian. What's your name?"

"Mark."

"It's nice to meet you, Mark."

"How'd you hurt your leg?"

Taken aback, Brian hesitated before answering. He'd forgotten how forthright children could be. "I hurt it in a car accident."

Mark's eyes widened. "Me, too. Was it a drunk driver?"

"No, it was my own fault."

"Will you get better?"

"I'm afraid this is as good as I'm going to get. I'll always need a cane."

"I got hit by a drunk driver when I was riding my bike home from school. Do you like horses?"

"I like them very much." Brian followed

181

the abrupt change of subject easily.

"Does anyone make fun of you because you can't ride?" Mark's dejected tone told Brian how much the earlier gibe had hurt.

Brian let the group move farther ahead. "I don't pay any attention to them if they do. Besides, being handicapped doesn't mean you can't ride a horse."

Catching Lindsey's eye, he motioned for her to continue with her tour. She nodded and began walking.

"All our tack repairs are done here in the leather shop. This is Corporal Shane Ross. He's going to explain the different types of leather we use and show you how we repair our harnesses," Lindsey said.

Lindsey stepped aside as the group crowded into the small room where Shane sat behind a large sewing machine. She walked back to where Brian had stopped pushing Mark.

Looking up with a mixture of disbelief and interest, Mark asked, "How can someone like me ride a horse?"

"I have a friend who runs a riding stable just for kids with disabilities. She has special saddles that will hold you strapped in place. Her horses are very gentle. All kinds of kids learn to ride there."

"Is it far away?" Mark's tone was wistful.

"It's only a half-hour drive from here. Why don't I give you my card. Have your parents call me and I'll tell them all about it."

"I don't know. Mom is funny about me doing stuff."

"Tell her that it's a very safe place and they have trained therapists there."

"Okay."

Lindsey dropped to one knee beside the boy. "How would you like to meet one of our horses up close and personal?"

He nodded eagerly. "That would be totally sweet."

"Good." She sent a questioning look at Brian. He nodded his approval.

"Right this way." Standing, she led them to Dakota's stall and opened the door.

Brian maneuvered the chair into the stall and Lindsey closed the door, shutting him and the boy inside. Dakota limped a few steps forward to investigate his visitors.

Mark held out one hand. "Come here, fella."

Lowering his head, Dakota sniffed at the boy's hand and then took another step closer so that Mark could pet the side of his face.

"What's wrong with him?" Mark gestured toward the cast.

"He broke his ankle and Dr. Brian fixed it

for him," Lindsey said from the doorway.

Mark looked up with interest. "You're a horse doctor?"

Brian nodded. "I'm a veterinary surgeon and I specialize in horses."

"That's tight, dude."

Brian glanced back at Lindsey. She grinned. "That means he thinks you have a cool job."

"Oh."

"We should get on with the tour," she said, holding open the door.

"Aw, do we have to?"

"I think we should." Brian waited until the boy said goodbye to Dakota and then pushed his chair out of the stall.

Outside the leather shop, he waited until the rest of the children came out and then followed the group and listened intently as Lindsey talked about the unit's job, their performances and the history of Fort Riley. It was obvious by the way she answered the children's questions that she enjoyed sharing her knowledge.

It wasn't until the last child was herded onto the bus and the vehicle pulled away that he saw her sag with relief and rub her arm.

"Are you hurting?"

"A little. Tell me more about the riding

stable for disabled children." They began walking back into the barn.

"It isn't just for children. Hearts and Horses is run by a woman I met when I treated one of her horses for colic. What she does is called hippotherapy."

"What is that exactly?"

"Hippotherapy uses the movement of the horse as a treatment in physical, occupational and speech therapy for people living with disabilities. It has been shown to improve their muscle tone, balance, coordination and motor development, as well as emotional well-being."

"That sounds like you have some firsthand experience."

"I volunteer at Hearts and Horses on the last Saturday of each month. It's a great way to spend an afternoon."

"I've heard of places like that, but I didn't know there were any near here."

"Actually, there are a half dozen such stables in the eastern part of Kansas. Some are members of the American Hippotherapy Association. Others belong to NARHA, the North American Riding for the Handicapped Association."

"I wonder if something like that would help my brother?"

"Every case is different, but didn't you

say he lived in Washington, D.C.? I know they have a center that works with veterans."

"I'll tell my sister-in-law to look into it. I think it would do Danny a world of good to be around horses again.

"Places like that would need very calm horses. We have a horse named Tiger who is getting ready to retire. I'll mention your friend's place to the Captain. Tiger might be a good fit for that kind of work."

"They also need trained volunteers to work with the children. Unfortunately, both good horses and volunteers are in short supply."

"That's a shame. I could see how eager Mark was to ride and yet how guarded he was about expressing his desire. I know it was because he was afraid of being disappointed."

"You should have children of your own," Brian said.

The second the words were out of his mouth he knew it was the wrong thing to say. It was very personal comment. He glanced at her to see her reaction. Other than looking bemused, she didn't seem upset by his odd statement.

"I'm afraid children aren't on my agenda for a quite a few more years."

Not exactly sure why he felt compelled to

press the issue, he said, "Agendas can change."

"Yes, they can, but I don't have a reason to change mine."

"I forgot. The army is your life. Is that enough?"

She cast a sideways glance at him. "I've always thought it would be."

He decided to change the subject. "I haven't seen Karen for a while. How is she?"

"Karen's fine. She's gone home for the holidays, but she is actually thinking of moving here and attending college next semester. She wants to become a grief counselor."

Brian looked down and used the tip of his cane to draw circles in the dirt. His family in Montana had tried to get him to see a grief counselor after Emily's death, but he had refused. He deserved the pain his grief brought. "What do you think of the idea?"

"Karen has a good heart and a great faith in God. I think she is taking my brother's tragedy and turning it into something positive. I really respect her for that."

He considered the idea that he hadn't allowed anything positive to come from Emily's death. He had wanted to stay wrapped up in his grief, but was he doing an injustice to Emily's memory?

He cocked his head to one side as he studied the woman who seemed so in control of her life.

"You did a good job with those kids today. Keeping a bunch of ten-year-olds interested in history for an hour is no easy feat."

She patted the holster at her side. "I wouldn't attempt it if I wasn't armed."

"I don't believe that for a minute."

She held up her free hand in a gesture of surrender. "Okay, you've found me out. I like kids. Arrest me."

Her smile was so adorable that he leaned in and kissed her.

CHAPTER TEN

Lindsey was so startled by Brian's kiss that she froze for an instant. Her next thought was how right it felt.

Abruptly, he took a step back. He looked as surprised as she was. She smiled shyly and touched her fingers to her lips.

Without a word, he began walking again. Not understanding exactly what was going on, she followed, perplexed by his silence.

"Brian, wait. Would you like to talk about what just happened?"

He stopped and faced her. "I'm sorry, I don't know what came over me."

Disappointment followed close on the heels of his words. "That is not exactly what a woman likes to hear after a man kisses her."

"You're a very attractive woman, but that isn't any excuse. I was way out of line. It won't happen again."

"So I guess we're clear on that?" About as

clear as mud, she decided.

"Absolutely clear. I value your friendship and I admire you as a person. I hope my lapse won't affect how we work together."

"Of course not." She had no idea what else to say.

"Good. That's good," he muttered.

At the barn door, Shane stood waiting for them. "I heard you needed some help with your X-ray equipment."

Brian nodded. "If you'll come with me, I'll show you what I need." The two of them walked to Brian's truck.

Lindsey entered the barn and walked into Dakota's stall. She began rubbing his cheek. Glancing around to make sure she was alone, she leaned forward and whispered in the horse's ear. "Brian just kissed me."

A happy glow swelled from within and she couldn't keep her smile contained any longer.

"As kisses go, it was pretty nice until he opened his mouth and began apologizing."

Her glow dimmed by several watts. He had certainly backpedaled quickly enough. Obviously she shouldn't read more into it, but she wouldn't mind if it happened again. She had begun to care a lot for Brian, but it was foolhardy to think that anything could come of those feelings. No, the best thing would be to put the episode firmly out of her mind.

If only it hadn't been such a nice kiss.

In a few minutes, Shane came in carrying several black cases. He and Brian were laughing about something and her heart quivered at the sound. Putting his kiss out of her mind wouldn't be easy.

Brian produced a tall block of wood from one case. "Lindsey, can you put this under his hoof, please?"

He was all business again. She did as he asked and tried to be as professional as possible. "Yes, sir."

"Now that Dakota is doing so well, you'll be seeing less of me. Once a week should be often enough for follow-up visits. My students can handle those."

"We've gotten kinda used to your company, Doc," Shane drawled from the stable door.

Lindsey realized with sudden clarity that Brian might simply fade out of her life the way numerous other friends had done over the years. Dakota was the reason they had spent so many hours together. When the horse was healed, their paths might never cross again. The happy glow she had been basking in went out like the flip of a switch.

Brian soon had his portable X-ray machine set up. By positioning Dakota's hoof on a block of wood to raise it off the ground, they were able to get the views Brian wanted while Lindsey kept the horse still by talking to him and scratching him behind his ear.

Shane watched from outside the stall. "Do you have big plans for Christmas, Doc?"

"No. I usually take call so that the other staff with families can have the day off."

"You're welcome to join us for dinner," Lindsey offered, and then thought of slapping her forehead with her hand. Would he think she was desperately trying to hold on to the relationship?

"Sure," Shane chimed in. "We're on duty, too. We usually get together in the ready room and bring in all the fixings."

Brian slanted a look at Lindsey. "Will you be doing the cooking?"

Her heart lightened at the sight of the humor glinting in his eyes. He was thinking about her burnt cookies. She grinned back. "No, my contribution will be two pumpkins pies from the commissary — already baked."

"I don't know. I hate to intrude on your party."

"You won't be intruding, Doc," Shane assured him. "After all you've done for Dakota, you're practically a member of the unit yourself."

"Thanks, I'll think about it."

"You could bring Isabella along," Lindsey suggested with a cheeky grin. "Dakota has been missing her."

Now that was desperate, but if it enticed him to come to dinner, she didn't care.

"I think she's been missing him, too. At least, she has been pouting about something."

"Who's Isabella?" Shane asked.

Lindsey winked at Brian. "She's Dakota's new friend, and she's as cute as a bunny."

Shane looked interested. "Is she that pretty blond secretary at the clinic?"

Brian shook his head. "She much cuter than Jennifer."

Sending him a chiding look, Lindsey said, "Oh, I'm going to tell Jennifer you said that."

His eyes widened in mock alarm. "Please don't. I shudder to think what she might do to me."

"All right, I won't squeal on you if you promise to join us for dinner on Christmas Day."

"Barring the need for my services at the clinic, I promise to try."

"We plan on eating about six, and don't

feel that you have to bring something. We'll have more than enough."

"I'll keep that in mind."

Lindsey grinned as she rubbed Dakota's neck. Suddenly, this holiday had become something special to look forward to, and Brian was the reason.

Christmas morning dawned bright and clear with just enough bite to the cold air to remind Brian that winter had arrived. As he scraped the frost from his truck's windshield, he still hadn't decided whether to accept Lindsey's invitation to dinner.

He tried telling himself that she had only offered out of kindness. It certainly couldn't be construed as a date even if it was a dinner invitation. After all, a half dozen other men would be there, too. He would go, and he would give her the present he had found for her. The trinket had caught his eye in the window of a gift shop downtown. The moment he saw it, he knew Lindsey would love it.

On the drive to the clinic with Isabella beside him, he passed one of the local churches. The tall white spire silhouetted against the clear blue sky looked Christmas-card perfect. The parking lot was already filling with early worshippers.

Lindsey would be at the base chapel this morning.

He envied her certainty, her belief in God's love above all else. Brian knew his heart was made of weaker clay. He had turned his back on God after Emily's death. He didn't expect his feelings would change anytime soon. He drove past the church without stopping, but the image of Lindsey bowing her head to pray stayed with him. That and the memory of their kiss.

Suddenly, he began to think of all the reasons he shouldn't go to Christmas dinner. One by one they crowded into his mind. He didn't belong to their group. He was an outsider invited out of charity. His presence would put a damper on their camaraderie and fun. His gift would seem too personal. The more he thought about it, the more certain he became — he wouldn't go.

Although the clinic was officially closed and he could have taken call from home, he decided to go in to catch up on some work. No holiday was complete without someone needing a vet in a hurry. If he was at the clinic already, it would speed up his response time. Throughout the day he glanced frequently at the clock. By noon he hadn't seen a single patient or taken a single call.

His conference presentation had been worked and reworked until he couldn't stand looking at the numbers and slides another minute.

Around two o'clock he decided there wasn't any reason his holiday should turn into a total waste. He could enjoy a meal that wasn't takeout or warmed up in a microwave for a change. He didn't have to stay long and make small talk. He would go.

As the afternoon dragged on, he finished reviewing a stack of odds and ends of paperwork, checked the clock, and then his watch a half dozen times. Isabella did nothing but nap in her box so he didn't even have her antics to help pass the time. After sharpening all his pencils and straightening his desk, he checked the clock again. It was four-fifteen and he finally made up his mind.

He wasn't going.

At five-thirty he closed the clinic doors and carried Isabella to his truck. Setting her in her carrier, he climbed in and shut the door. With his hands on the steering wheel, he sat in his parking space without starting the engine. It had turned colder outside. Gray clouds had moved in and occasional snowflakes drifted earthward to vanish as

196

soon as they touched anything. It might be snowing, but the forecast was only calling for a trace of the white stuff.

"We should get going," he told Isabella. But he didn't move. The thought of heading home to an empty house tonight left him feeling forlorn.

I don't have to be alone tonight.

He had spent so much time avoiding people that he wasn't sure he knew how to interact in a purely social situation. Especially with a woman as lovely and lively as Lindsey. The last thing he wanted to do was to stir up feelings that were better left buried.

Who was he kidding? Those feelings had been coming to life since the first day he met Lindsey Mandel — and it scared him half to death.

Lindsey's anticipation slowly seeped away as six o'clock, then six-thirty slipped past. She tried to enjoy the feast brought together by the men, but disappointment made even the cranberry salad taste bland.

Why hadn't Brian come?

Maybe he'd had an emergency surgery. If she knew that for certain she might be able to enjoy what was left of the day, but something told her he wasn't tied up at work. Some small part of her knew that Brian didn't want to see her. He had kissed her, but it had meant nothing to him. If only it had meant nothing to her, too.

"How about some dessert, Lindsey?" Lee held out a paper plate loaded with a huge slice of pie and mounds of whipped cream.

She held up her hand. "No, thanks. I'm full."

"Full? You hardly touched a bite of the Captain's smoked turkey."

"I ate my share. Just because I can't put away as much chow as you do is no reason to imply that I'm finicky."

"Leave her alone," Shane said as he snagged the plate from Lee's hand. "She has to watch her girlish figure."

He forked a piece into his mouth as he whirled away from Lee's attempt to grab the plate back. "Hey, fix your own!"

Lindsey smiled at their foolishness but didn't feel like joining in as they returned to the folding chairs positioned in front of the small portable TV Avery had provided for the evening. Instead, she began to gather up the dirty paper plates and toss them in the trash.

"Is something wrong, Lindsey?" Captain Watson moved to help her clean up.

"No, sir."

"I thought maybe your arm was hurting."

"It aches, especially with the weather turning colder."

"Are you getting any feeling back in your hand?"

"A little, but I still don't have any kind of grip."

"Dakota looks like he's doing well."

"I think so, too. How are you doing, sir?" She had heard through the grapevine that he and his wife had separated.

He looked at her sharply. "You mean on my first major holiday as a divorced man?"

"Something like that. Not that I want to pry."

"It's okay. No, it's been rough."

"Do you have kids?"

"Two. My son is fifteen and my daughter just turned thirteen. I've been gone for so many holidays during my career that I doubt they even miss me tonight."

"I'm sure that isn't true."

"Maybe not, but I wasn't there much for my kids when they were little. I can't blame them if they ignore me now."

"Don't let them. Nothing is more important than your family. Pick up the phone and give them a call. Let them know you care."

Indecision crossed his face, followed by a

growing look of determination. "Thanks, I think I will."

As he walked away to his office, Lindsey thought back to all the times her father had been gone when she was little. He had missed more than his share of Christmas days even after their mother left. That had left Lindsey, Danny and Karen to fend for themselves. They had worked hard at making presents for each other and even harder at sneaking around to fill stockings when no one was looking. They had made the holidays something special for one another.

Did her father regret those missed opportunities the way Captain Watson did? She wanted to believe that was true. There was really only one way to find out. Talking to her father wouldn't change the past, but it might make the future brighter for both of them.

Pulling out her cell phone, she walked into the hall away from the noise and laughter and dialed her father's number. The least she could do was follow the advice she gave out so freely.

He answered on the second ring. "Hello?"

"Dad, it's Lindsey."

"Lindsey, honey, it's so good to hear your voice."

She relaxed at the sound of his genuine

happiness. "It's good to hear you, too. I wanted to wish you a Merry Christmas, only . . . it doesn't feel right to be celebrating."

"I know." His voice became choked with emotion. "But life goes on."

"Yes, it does." She wanted to cry away the pain she had been holding inside. She wanted to feel the comfort of her father's arms around her.

After a long pause, he asked, "How's your arm?" His voice sounded more in control.

"I got my cast off last week, but my arm is still pretty weak and I can't use my hand much. Will you be coming to the parade?" she asked quickly.

"Of course. You'll still be riding, won't you?"

"Yes, Dakota and I will be there."

"So the horse is doing better?"

"Karen told you?"

"She did. I agree with you. As long as things look like they're going to work out, I don't think we should tell Danny. The last thing he needs is to start fretting about the animal. Are things looking good? Because if they aren't, I can't keep that from him."

"Dr. Cutter says Dakota may get his cast off in a few days."

"That's good, but you won't be carrying

the flag if you can't use your hand."

"I haven't given up. I still have time to get better. I do my exercises, and I'm as determined as Danny to get in shape for the big day."

"That's my girl. Make your old man proud and show the world what we Mandels are made of. I know Danny is looking forward to seeing the pair of you."

"I won't disappoint him or you."

"Have you talked to him lately?"

"I called them last night, why?"

"Did he tell you that with his tracheotomy capped off, he can stay off his ventilator for eight hours?"

"Yes, Abigail mentioned it."

"He's getting stronger every day and we have you to thank for that."

"Danny is doing the work, Dad."

"Yes, but Abigail and I both think you and that horse are the reason he's found the focus he needs. We both thank God that you have done this for him."

"He's my brother. I'd do anything for him."

"I know you would, honey."

She finished talking to her father and talked briefly with Karen, then ended the call. Stuffing her phone back in her pocket, she stared at the ceiling.

Please, Lord, let Dakota be healed enough to travel and let me be strong enough to hold the flag. I couldn't bear it if I had to let Danny down.

She had started to rejoin the men in front of the TV when a knock sounded at the front door. Hope sprang up in her heart. She pulled open the door and saw Brian standing in front of her. The darkness behind him was filled with soft, feathery snowflakes drifting down. It was a perfect Christmas evening.

Thank You, Lord, for bringing him here tonight.

"Merry Christmas," she said, knowing she had to be grinning from ear to ear.

"Merry Christmas." He held out a small red box with a silver bow. "This is for you."

She took the gift and clutched it close to her chest. She had a present for him, too, but it could wait until later. "Thank you. Come in. The guys are watching TV in the other room."

"Did I miss dinner?"

"I saved you a plate."

"Good, because I'm starved."

She looked behind him toward his truck. "Where is Isabella?"

He motioned with his head toward the stables. "I put her in with Dakota in his stall. I couldn't believe how excited she was to see him."

"The horse and the holiday hare. There's a children's story in that somewhere." Lindsey stepped back and allowed him to come inside.

Brian shook the snow from his black overcoat and hung it on an empty peg behind the door. He couldn't get over the way Lindsey stood watching him with that adorable, kissable smile on her face.

He smiled back. "Aren't you going to open your present?"

"Not yet. After you've had your dinner."

"All right, lead the way." He followed her into the crowded room where other members of the unit were gathered around the television set.

Shane noticed him first. "Hey, look who decided to join us. Have a seat, Doc. The game's tied and Baltimore has the ball on the six-yard line."

Lindsey pulled him by the arm toward a table set up in the opposite corner of the room. "After he gets a plate. Turkey or ham, Brian?"

"Both."

"Help yourself, we have plenty left."

After loading his plate, Brian took the seat Shane offered. Lindsey sat crossed-legged on the floor in front of him and it wasn't long until they were all engrossed in the football game.

The rapid-fire banter and good-natured teasing going on around him reminded Brian of his own family gatherings when he was a kid. Oddly enough, he didn't feel like an outsider amongst these people. They were all far from their families and homes. They were strangers joined together by the special bond of military service. He relaxed and joined in the chatter, adding his own armchair-coaching comments and rooting for the team opposite the one Lindsey urged on.

In the end, his team lost, but he didn't care. Watching Lindsey's brief victory jig was enough of a reward.

As the evening grew late, one by one the men left until only Shane, Avery and Lindsey remained. Brian wished them all goodnight and was headed toward the door and his coat when Lindsey rushed up beside him.

"I'll go with you to fetch Isabella."

"It may take two of us to pry her away from Dakota. Let me help you with your coat."

"Thanks." She turned around and slipped one arm into the heavy military-issue jacket he held. The other sleeve hung empty as he covered her sling.

"You need to button up. You'll catch cold running around like that." He pulled her jacket closed and began doing up the snaps.

"I can manage," she protested.

"So can I," he countered, and continued until he had the last one snapped beneath her chin. In the sudden stillness, he gazed down at her in wonder. His heart had been bound by grief for so long that he wasn't certain what he was feeling. He was only certain that this woman had somehow managed to work her way past that barrier and plant seeds of kindness and friendship. What, if anything, might grow from those seeds he had no way of knowing, but he was willing to wait and see.

He stepped back and opened the door. "It's getting late. I don't want to keep you up past your bedtime."

She wrinkled her nose. "Duty call does come early. Oh, wait a minute, I forgot something."

Hurrying down the hall, she vanished around the corner and reappeared a few seconds later with a bulge in one pocket. "Okay. Let's go round up the rabbit."

Outside, the air had turned colder and the snow had begun to accumulate on the cars.

A light dusting covered the ground, as well. Brian leaned on his cane heavily as they crossed the asphalt parking lot made slippery by the still-falling snow. Lindsey hurried on ahead. Brian was thankful she didn't seem to notice his difficult progress. He really disliked walking on slick surfaces. He hated knowing one slip might leave him unable to rise unaided.

Once inside the barn, he breathed a sigh of relief. Lindsey, a few yards down the aisle, was turning on the lights at Dakota's end of the stable. The commotion woke the other horses, who moved to hang their heads out the stall doors and check out their nighttime visitors.

Brian stopped to pet the onlookers as he made his way slowly over the rough cobblestones. "Merry Christmas, Trooper. Merry Christmas, Socks. Merry Christmas, Tiger."

"They all wish you a Merry Christmas, too," Lindsey said when he reached her side.

She nodded toward Dakota's stall. "You won't believe where your rabbit has decided to take a nap."

"Where?" He leaned over the half door to look inside. Dakota lay at the back of the stall with his legs folded under him. Isabella lay perched on his broad back sound asleep with her head pillowed on her front paws and her long ears draped on either side of them.

Brian glanced at Lindsey and they both began to laugh. "You are right," he said. "This really has the makings of a great children's story."

"Before you go, I want you to have this." She pulled a black box from her pocket. "It's actually from all of us, including Dakota, but I picked it out."

"Thank you, but you didn't have to get me anything. The turkey and dressing was more than enough." He took the box from her and opened it. Inside lay a gold pocket watch engraved with a U.S. flag.

She leaned forward eagerly. "Turn it over and read the inscription."

He did as she suggested. " 'To Dr. Cutter with endless gratitude. The CGMCG.' "

"I hope you don't mind the initials. Writing out the Commanding General's Mounted Color Guard would take up most of a large wall clock."

"This is beautiful. Thank you."

"I'm glad you like it."

"I do. This makes two terrific presents this year."

"What was your other one?"

"The equine ambulance company called the day before yesterday. They're loaning us their newest model for our conference."

"Brian, that's great. I know how much it means to you."

"True, but I'm still a little disappointed."

She cocked her head to one side. "Why?"

"I didn't get to see you open your gift."

With a saucy smile, she pulled his box from the depth of her pocket. "I didn't want to open it in front of the guys."

"Open it now," he suggested quietly.

"I can't get the ribbon off one-handed, and I'm sure you don't want to watch me try to do it with my teeth."

"Let me help." He hung his cane over the stall door and took the gift from her. Carefully, he worked off the silver satin ribbon and bow without breaking it, then held out the box.

She lifted the top and gasped with delight. "Brian, it's beautiful."

With the utmost care, she lifted out a small delicate snow globe. Inside the glass dome a bay horse pranced between snow-laden pine trees. She shook it and sent the glittering snowflakes whirling about him. "It looks just like Dakota!"

"There are fifteen bays in the stable. How can you tell that it looks like Dakota?"

"Because it's my present and I say it's Dakota." She shook it again and the snow whirled faster.

"I'm glad you like it."

"It will always remind me that your presence with us tonight was a special Christmas blessing."

More than anything, he wanted to kiss her again, but something held him back. Some part of him didn't trust the new emotions churning inside him the way her miniature blizzard swirled inside the glass bubble.

He said, "It's getting late. I should get going."

"Of course." Did she look disappointed? She turned away before he could read her face.

He opened the stall door and stepped inside. Lindsey followed him and spoke softly to Dakota. She squatted by his head while Brian plucked his pet from her perch and cradled her in his arm.

"I'll be back the day after tomorrow without the rabbit. If Dakota's X-rays look good, we'll get his cast off."

She stood and shoved her free hand in her coat pocket. "Once that's done, will you still need to see him?"

"I'll need monthly follow-ups for at least six months to document his recovery."

"And after that?"

"You won't see me ever again." He tried

to make it sound like a joke, but his words fell flat.

She stepped close and he didn't move away. She pulled her hand from her pocket and laid it on his chest as she gazed into his eyes. "I hope that isn't true, because I would miss you."

Raising on tiptoe, she brushed her lips softly against his.

CHAPTER ELEVEN

For the next day and a half, Brian couldn't put Lindsey's kiss out of his head. The scene played over and over in his mind and left him wondering constantly what he should have done or said differently. Anything might have been better than standing like a mute statue while every trace of common sense and logic evaporated from his brain, leaving nothing but the yearning to gather her close in his arms.

At least he hadn't done that. Instead, she left him without a word, but her shy smile and knowing glance made it pretty obvious that the next move would be up to him.

So exactly what would he say to her today?

Packing his equipment into his truck, he prepared to go and take another set of X-rays of Dakota. In spite of the setbacks, the horse's recovery had progressed much better than he had hoped. His combination of arthrodesis and bone-growth-gene therapy certainly looked like a success. The first draft of his report on the procedure sat on his desk. Having serial X-rays and a sound horse to back up his hypothesis would certainly make for a more interesting presentation at the conference.

He should be happy that the horse's recovery was almost complete, but he wasn't. Once Dakota's cast was off, Brian knew he wouldn't be seeing Lindsey unless he decided to become involved in a relationship with her.

Shoving an awkward piece of equipment into place, he tried not to think about her — about the softness of her lips or about the way she made him feel. He didn't have time for a relationship. The more he tried to convince himself that was true, the more often thoughts of Lindsey intruded into his working day. When he was alone, it was even worse.

He stowed the last X-ray cassette in the truck and closed the door. He knew by the tenderness of her kiss that Lindsey had grown very fond of him. He wanted to be fair to her. She needed to understand that he couldn't give her more than friendship. Not even if he found himself wondering exactly where *more* would take them.

He moved to the driver's side and yanked

open the door. It was with mixed emotions that he headed toward the Fort Riley stables.

Lindsey coasted through her morning duties on the same cushion of air that had held her up since Christmas night. Everything seemed right with the world and she couldn't stop smiling. She was in love with Brian Cutter.

She hadn't planned it. She still didn't know how they could make their different situations work, but she knew that he was the man of her heart.

It was a secret she hadn't told anyone. Karen had returned from Washington the night before, but the feeling was just too new and special to share.

Humming her favorite Christmas tune, she carried a bucket of grain to each of the horses and the mules in the barn and made sure that they all had water. The sprinkling of snow that had helped to make Christmas night so special had quickly melted. Today's bright sunshine would soon dry the lingering mud. On one hand, Lindsey would have liked the Christmas white to last a little longer, but the horses were eager to get out into the open pastures and she didn't relish the idea of brushing down a muddy herd when they came back in.

As she worked, she kept glancing out the stable doors toward the parking lot. Brian should be here soon.

Dakota whinnied loudly and she turned to him with a chuckle. "Are you anxious to see Brian, too?"

Shane came down the aisle pushing a wheelbarrow loaded with straw. He set down his load and rubbed Dakota's forehead. "I think he's anxious to get his cast off."

"I know exactly how he feels. I couldn't wait to get mine off, but I hope he does better than I did."

"You're getting better."

She massaged her hand in the sling. "I can move my fingers a little, but my arm is still weak. I have a doctor's appointment at four o'clock. I'm hoping he'll let me out of this thing."

"Hey, your boyfriend just pulled up."

She spun around to peer out into the bright sunshine. "Brian's here? Where?"

Shane lifted the handles of the wheelbarrow and pushed it past her. "No denials today? Do I hear wedding bells, Sergeant?"

Grinning back at him, she shook her head. "Don't be silly. We haven't even had a first date."

"If he doesn't snap you up, he's a fool."

"What a nice thing to say. Thank you, Shane."

"I mean it. Morning, Doc," he called out.

"Good morning, Corporal." Lindsey watched Brian make his way toward them and she drank in the sight of him. He was dressed in a dark maroon sweater over faded jeans and his hair looked as unruly as ever. She resisted the urge to comb it out with her fingers. He stopped a few feet away from her. She wondered if he was as delighted to see her as she was to see him.

Shane glanced at the two of them, then chuckled as he pushed his burden outside. "I'll be back to give you a hand with Dakota in five minutes."

Brian looked down at the cobblestone floor. "How are you?"

"I'm good. How are you?"

"Fine. Lindsey, I'd like to speak to you in private."

"I'd like that, too." Avery and Lee walked by a second later. She tried to look nonchalant as she smiled and nodded at them.

Once they were out of earshot, Lindsey said, "It seems privacy is hard to come by around here, today."

Brian seemed ill at ease, too, and she found that adorable. Love left her feeling shy but happy to be in his company.

Just then two soldiers came in with their saddles headed for the leather shop. Any hopes she had of finding time alone with Brian vanished. Knowing that they could be overheard, she said, "I mentioned your friend's place, Hearts and Horses, to Captain Watson as a possible retirement place for Tiger."

"What did he think?"

"He's interested. He wants to talk to you about it and perhaps have us visit the facility. I know you said you volunteered there on the last Saturday of each month, but will you be going out there this Saturday?"

"They'll be closed because of the holidays, but I did promise my friend that I would be there next Saturday. I should stay home and work on my lecture, but I really hate to disappoint any of the kids. Do you remember Mark, the boy in the wheelchair from your tour group?"

"Of course."

"My friend told me his mother enrolled him as a Christmas present."

"That's great. I know he's going to love it."

Shane came back into the barn followed by a dozen unit members. "I brought the cheering section, Doc."

"Then let's get started."

With the help of Shane and another soldier, Brian soon had his X-ray machine in place. That left Lindsey free to watch him work. He didn't allow his stiff leg to hamper his job. Instead, he seemed to accomplish things with a minimum of motion, as if he had learned to make every move count.

"It will take a few minutes to print these," he said as he exited the stall and headed for his truck. More of the men from the unit had gathered in the barn.

When Brian walked back in, Captain Watson was with him. As they stopped in front of the group, Brian held the black-and-white film aloft. "The cast can come off."

A cheer went up and everyone began pounding each other on the back, shaking hands with Brian and giving Lindsey heartfelt hugs.

The Captain was the one who asked the question they all were wondering about. "Does this mean Dakota can travel to Washington, D.C.?"

"No, it means he can begin his rehabilitation. He'll need to be hand walked for short periods only. I'll give you a schedule of times to start with and then we'll see how he progresses. I want to be notified at the first sign of any lameness."

Lindsey clasped her hands together in front of her. "But there's still hope that he'll be able to make the trip, isn't there?"

"A slim hope, I'm afraid."

"That's good enough for us, isn't it?" Lindsey asked the men around her. They responded with resounding affirmatives.

"We have faith in you and in Dakota, Dr. Cutter," Lindsey said. "He's going."

Brian studied the determined and hopeful faces around him and decided not to press the issue. No one here would endanger the horse by insisting he make the long trip if he wasn't ready when the time came.

"Before I remove his cast, he'll need new shoes put on. The ones he has on now will be too tall and I don't want him to experience an uneven gait."

"We have our farrier standing by, Doctor," Captain Watson assured him. "It shouldn't take long to change them."

Once the new shoes were in place, Dakota stood quiet and calm as his cast was removed. Brian stepped back and asked Lindsey to lead him around the stall. At first, Dakota balked, but with some easy coaxing, he finally took his first steps. Without the weight of the cast, he raised his newly freed leg higher than the other several times but soon seemed to realize he didn't need to.

"He has a slight limp, but I think he's going to do fine," Brian said to Captain Watson as both men watched the horse closely.

"You've done great work and the army is grateful."

"I'm the one who is grateful, Captain. You allowed me to enroll him as my first patient in my clinical trials. His success will certainly add weight to my upcoming conference presentation. He may even make more funding available for the study. I can't tell you how important that is to me."

"We wish you all the best."

"Thank you, sir."

The Captain crossed his arms over his chest. "I wonder if we might ask one more favor of you?"

"Certainly, if I can."

"Sergeant Mandel mentioned you know of a riding stable for handicapped children that might be interested in Tiger. He's extremely well trained, as are all our horses, but I'd like your opinion on his suitability before I officially ask for his release from service."

"I'll be happy to look him over and make sure he's sound, but the only way to tell how he'll do is to expose him to the new environment. We'll need to see how he reacts to wheelchairs, noisy children, unsteady riders, any number of unexpected occurrences. Hearts and Horses has an evaluation program and I know they would welcome the opportunity to see if Tiger would be right for them."

"We can do that. Sergeant Mandel, assign a detail to arrange transport for Tiger to the Hearts and Horses facility. At the facility's convenience, of course. We'll go ahead with his evaluation, but make sure they know that he won't be available until our return from Washington, D.C. I don't want our senior member to miss this Inaugural parade. Fifteen years of service has earned him the right to participate."

"Yes, sir."

Brian felt the sensation of his beeper vibrating on his belt. He pulled it from his clip and read the message. He was wanted back at the hospital, but he still hadn't had a chance to speak to Lindsey in private. He looked around and saw she was talking to Shane and Avery. It seemed that he wasn't going to get a chance today.

Maybe it was for the best. Now that they wouldn't be seeing each other so often they could simply allow the relationship to fade. Besides, what if he had read more into her kiss than she meant?

No, he decided, not speaking to her was taking the coward's way out. He walked up beside her. "Lindsey, I've got to go."

"Now?" She couldn't have looked more disappointed if she had tried.

"I'm needed back at the clinic. Is there any way I could see you later this afternoon? I need to talk to you."

"Sure. I have to go into Manhattan tonight. Why don't I stop by the clinic later."

"That would be fine. If I'm not in surgery, we can get a cup of coffee or something." He wasn't happy with the way that sounded. It was too much like asking her for a date, but he had no way to change his words. Why couldn't a guy buy a verbal eraser?

"I'd like that. I'll drop by about five-thirty. Is that too late?"

"Five-thirty will be fine. See you then."

His emergency turned out to be a horse with a severe cut to its left hind leg. It took less than an hour to supervise while his fourth-year student stitched up the patient and another twenty minutes to update the owners and outline a plan of care. He had just finished his paperwork and was handing it to Jennifer to be filed at the front desk when he saw Lindsey coming in the front doors. His breath froze in his chest.

She paused inside the doorway and

slipped off her tan coat, then draped it over her arm. It was then that he noticed she wasn't wearing her sling. Smiling, she waved when she saw him.

She wore a dark green blouse with tiny flowers embroidered around the gathered neckline and on the short puff sleeves. A full black-and-green print skirt flared about her slim legs as she walked toward him. Dainty, high-heeled black shoes made those legs look even longer.

Jennifer pulled the file folder from his slack hand. "Wow. That is a big improvement over combat boots."

He couldn't have agreed more.

Lindsey stopped in front of him. Her bright smile turned his insides to pudding.

She said, "Hi. Am I too early? I can wait if you aren't finished with your work."

He found his voice and tried for a professional tone. "Ah, no, your timing is good. Why don't we just step into my office?"

"Okay."

He turned to his secretary. "Jennifer, hold my calls please."

"With pleasure." She winked.

He wanted to strangle her. Instead, he said, "Sergeant Mandel and I won't be long."

He allowed Lindsey to precede him down

the hall. As he opened the door for her, he spied his rabbit in the middle of his desk engaged in her forbidden activity.

"Isabella, put down that pencil!" Brian strode to the desk and pulled the prize from between her paws. He picked her up and sent Lindsey a defeated look.

"I've tried everything and I can't break her of getting into these."

He raised Isabella to eye level and scowled at her. "You are a bad bunny. Do not chew on my pencils."

Then, as if regretting his harsh words, he tucked her under his arm and stroked her head. Walking to the door, he opened it and called for Jennifer. She arrived and took one look at Isabella and the yellow paint flakes on her face and feet.

"Pencils again?"

"Will you put her in her outside kennel for me, please?"

"Of course. Come here, you naughty little girl," she cooed as she took the bunny from him. Ruffling the rabbit's fur, Jennifer continued to talk baby talk as she carried the offender away.

Lindsey watched the whole exchange, then raised one eyebrow. "Do you treat her that harshly each time she chews up a pencil?"

"I didn't think I was too harsh."

"You picked her up, petted her, gave her to Jennifer so that she could pet her and then sent her to the place she most likes to go — outside. In spite of all that she won't stop chewing your pencils. Will wonders never cease?"

Walking to the desk, she picked up his pencil cup, opened the deep drawer on the right-hand side of his desk and set the cup in it.

"Have you tried this?" She stared at him as she closed the drawer.

Brian pursed his lips searching for a good reply. None came to him. Feeling sheepish, he stepped closer. "Is your advice to simply remove the temptation?"

Oh, what a temptation this woman presented. Her bright eyes were brimming with mirth. The subtle scent of her perfume filled him with a desire to hold her close and breathe in the freshness she brought to his life just by being near.

"You're the animal specialist." Her sassy tone was almost too much. Calling on every ounce of self-control that he possessed, he resisted the urge to take her in his arms and kiss her. He didn't deserve to love another woman, but somehow Lindsey had a way of making him forget that fact.

Could that be the reason their paths had crossed? Was it time for him to move past the grief that had controlled his life until now?

He pulled open the drawer and set his cup back in its place in the center of his desk. "I like my pencils where they're easy to reach."

She grabbed a new one out of his cup and tapped it gently against her cheek. "I see."

He knew he was in trouble the moment he saw the mischievous glint in her eyes.

"So, is this what a girl has to do to get some attention from you?" She grinned and placed the pencil between her teeth.

Her playfulness melted the last of the icy barrier that enclosed his heart. Reaching up, he took the pencil from her and dropped it onto his desk, then he took her by the shoulders and drew her into his arms. She stepped into his embrace and lifted her face. Lowering his mouth to hers, he tasted again the poignant sweetness that was so uniquely her.

After a long second, he pulled away. Tucking her head under his chin, he drew a ragged breath. "I've been thinking about doing that all day."

"If I had known, I would have come sooner. Just don't start apologizing again."

"I won't."

"Good. You could give a girl a complex that way."

"Somehow, I don't see that happening to you. You're much too sure of yourself and your place in the world."

Resting in the comfort of his arms, Lindsey knew Brian was mistaken about that. She might sound sure of her plans, but more and more she had begun to question what she really wanted out of life. She had dismissed the idea of having a husband and children because she had seen how badly her parents had mismanaged their marriage. She never wanted to subject a child to that kind of pain. Only now, being held by Brian, she wondered if she had been wrong.

She drew back, determined to regroup her scattered wits. "I believe you asked me here for a reason. We seemed to have gotten sidetracked."

"It wasn't anything important, but I do owe you a cup of coffee."

"Yes, you do." She reluctantly stepped out of his embrace.

"We can make some here or we can go out to one of those trendy coffee shops that have sprung up all over town."

"Yours will be fine. It can't be worse than what Shane makes for us at the office."

"Don't be too sure about that. But you're

all dressed up. Are you certain you don't want to go out?"

"I'm dressed up because I have a Bible-study class in about half an hour."

"Is it on base?" He busied himself with filling the coffeemaker and adding heaping scoops of grounds to the filter.

"No, it's at Grayson Community Christian Church." She sat down on the sofa, remembering the gentle way he had cared for her the first time she had been in his office. So much about Brian Cutter was a contradiction. He often sounded gruff and uncaring, but the more she came to know him, the more certain she was that he was a man with a tender heart.

"I know that church. It's on the road that leads to my house."

"Is that where you worship?"

He paused in the act of pouring water into the coffeemaker. "I haven't been to church since my wife died."

"Did the two of you attend before that?"

"Emily was really involved with our church back home. She sang in the choir and helped out in the nursery. She even edited the newsletter for the pastor. She had such boundless energy. I attended when I could, but animals get sick and injured as much on Sunday as any other day. At least, that was the excuse I used."

"Why haven't you been back?"

"I blamed God for her death. I blamed myself. I can't get past the anger."

"Forgiveness is such a large part of our faith, Brian. You can't truly love someone else unless you first love yourself. And you can't truly forgive someone else unless you first forgive yourself."

He didn't answer her. He finished pouring in the water and pressed the on switch. She rose from the sofa and crossed to his side. Linking her arm through his, she laid her head on his shoulder. "Come with me tonight."

"To Bible-study class?"

"Yes."

"I don't know."

"Brian, we all struggle to find where we fit into God's plan, but if you aren't looking, you'll never find the answer."

"How can you be so sure that God *is* the answer?"

She straightened and cupped his cheek with her hand. "We use our head to make a lot of decisions in life, but some decisions have to be made with the heart. This is one of them. Do what your heart tells you is right."

He covered her hand with his own. "My

heart is telling me that kissing you again is the right thing to do."

"See, your heart knows best," she whispered as she leaned toward him. Their lips met and the kiss was everything she had dreamed it would be. After a long moment, she pulled away and placed her palm over his lips.

"Okay, my head is telling me that I'm going to be late for class."

He kissed her palm, then drew her hand away from his mouth. "Smart, as well as beautiful. I never thought I could feel this way about someone again. I'm not sure this is real."

"It's real enough for me. I care for you deeply, Brian."

"And I care for you, so where exactly does this leave us?"

"I'm not sure." There were so many things to consider, but with happiness zinging through her veins, she couldn't think of anything but how wonderful it felt to be in his arms.

"Lindsey, I want to keep seeing you."

Smiling softly, she said, "That sounds like an excellent start."

"I want to know everything there is to know about you."

"Everything?"

He pulled her close and kissed the tip of her nose. "Everything," he whispered.

"I'm just an ordinary girl."

"Who happens to be a sergeant in the U.S. Army."

"Is that a problem?" She held her breath, hoping he didn't see her career as a road-block to this budding relationship.

"I don't know. Have you thought about leaving the service?"

She frowned and leaned back to study his face. "Are you asking me to do that?"

"I'm asking if you have considered it."

"I will admit that I've been toying with the idea, but it's something I would have to give a lot of thought."

"Of course. I don't want to rush you or pressure you into making a decision you'll regret."

"Thank you."

"I know that I want to see more of you. I want to be a part of your life."

"My life includes church, Brian. Can you accept that?"

"I'll try. I can't promise anything more than that."

A small voice in the back of her mind pointed out that he hadn't mentioned the word *love*. She ignored it by telling herself that things were happening too fast, for both of them.

CHAPTER TWELVE

Lindsey let herself into her apartment a little after ten-thirty that night. She tried to be quiet, but Karen was a light sleeper.

"Lindsey, is that you?" she asked from the sofa.

"Yes, I'm home. Go back to sleep."

"I will, but I'm supposed to give you a message. Dad wants you to call him."

"Tonight?"

Karen sat up and stretched. "He said whenever you got home. You know how he likes to watch the late shows. He'll be up."

"Did he say what he wanted? Is something wrong?"

"I don't think so. I got the feeling he wanted to discuss your next duty station."

"Great. After years of ignoring me, he suddenly wants to pick my career moves." She tossed her purse on the overstuffed chair in the corner and hung her coat in the closet.

"He's trying to be a better father, Lindsey.

Danny's injury was a wake-up call for Dad. He knows he hasn't always been there for you. Give him a chance."

"You're right, I'm sorry. It's just that he was always so eager to hear about what Danny was doing, but I got the feeling that he thought my duties weren't important."

"You've been invited to participate in the Inaugural Parade. How many people ever get the chance to do something like that?"

"I know. I'm thankful for the opportunity, but it's not because of anything I've done. Don't get me wrong. I'm delighted to be able to honor Danny and all the other men and women who have given so much for us, but it isn't like I've done anything special."

"It's because of you that Danny is working so hard in rehab. It's only because of you that the army accepted Dakota. Don't sell yourself short. What you do counts for a lot."

"Thanks."

"You're home late — did your class run over?"

Lindsey settled on the sofa beside Karen. She needed to share her happiness with someone. "Brian went with me to Bible study tonight. Afterward, we stopped and had a cup of coffee together."

"That's wonderful! Did he like it? What

did he say?"

"He said, 'Double-chocolate latte, no foam.' Or something like that, and he really seemed to enjoy it."

Karen growled as she punched Lindsey's shoulder. "I don't mean what did he say about the coffee. I meant, what did he say about the class?"

Lindsey rubbed the tender spot. "Careful. That's my only good arm."

"It won't be good for long unless you tell me everything."

"He said it gave him a lot to think about."

"That's great. I'll pray that he finds his way back to God."

"I'm praying for that, too."

"And I'll add a special request that he ask you out on another date."

"It wasn't exactly a date."

"Close enough. Oh, I can't wait until Danny meets Brian. I think they'll like each other."

Lindsey took her sister's hand and squeezed it. "They will, won't they? I'm so in love. Does it show?"

"Yes. Oh, girl, I'm so happy for you." She enveloped Lindsey in a quick, hard hug.

Lindsey returned the hug. "Thanks, sis."

Karen drew back. "Now go call Dad and let me get back to sleep."

Lindsey wanted to talk about Brian all night long, but she kept the rest of her happiness in check. "All right. Good night, kid."

Alone in her bedroom, Lindsey sat on the side of her bed and dialed her father's number. He picked up on the first ring.

"Hi, Dad. It's me. Did I wake you?"

"No, I was up."

"What did you need?"

"Nothing really. I just wanted you to know that we plan to be in front of the Hoover Building so you'll know where to look for us."

"I'm glad you're going to be there."

"I wouldn't miss it. My daughter in the Inaugural parade. Makes me mighty proud just to think about it."

She had longed to hear those words from him for so many years that she could barely speak. "Thanks, Dad. How is Danny?"

"He's making good progress. How's the arm?"

"I'm out of my sling. I can make a fist now, but my grip is still weak. I don't know if I'll be able to hold a flag."

"You'll be ready. I know you will. Say, your enlistment will be up soon, won't it?"

"I've got two months left."

"How long are you reenlisting for?"

It was the question she least wanted to

hear. "I'm not sure."

"If you give them eight years you can just about pick any billet you want. I've got friends here in Washington. A Pentagon job isn't out of the question. That way you'd be close to Danny."

Eight years — it sounded like an eternity. For the first time she gave voice to the thought that had been roaming around in the back of her mind. "There isn't anything that says I have to reenlist."

"What? Mandels have always been soldiers. It's in our blood." He sounded appalled that she would even suggest not reenlisting.

"It was just a thought."

"I know you've taken Danny's injury hard, but think how he would feel if you quit because of him. You're not going to leave the service. Not my daughter. I raised you better than that."

"Karen isn't in the service." Lindsey felt a fleeting touch of envy for the way Karen had always stood her ground on the issue.

"No, that one takes after her mother's side of the family for sure, but I haven't given up on her. You, on the other hand, take after me. You'd be lost in civilian life."

Maybe he was right. She had wanted to be a soldier all her life. Just as she had wanted to earn her father's respect all her life, she thought with sudden clarity. The two issues were so closely intertwined she wasn't sure she could tell which was which, not that it mattered. But he was right about one thing — she couldn't have Danny thinking she left the service because of him.

"It was just a thought, Dad. I'm sorry I said anything."

"That's more like it. You had me worried."

"If you had left the army, would it have made a difference with you and Mom?"

He was silent for a few seconds, then he said, "There were a lot of things wrong with our marriage, Lindsey. Being in the service was only part of it. Your mother was miserable in our situation, and I knew I would be miserable if I got out of the army. In the end, we did what made us both less miserable. I'm sorry you kids were caught in the middle."

"You did your best, Dad."

"And it must have been good enough. Two of my children joined up and followed in my footsteps. A man couldn't ask for more than that." His obvious pride came shining through in his words.

"I'll give some thought to working in Washington, D.C."

"You do that. Wherever you decide to go,

I know you'll make me proud."

Tears pricked her eyelids. "Thanks, Dad."

"The army will take you places, kid. It's a great life."

The army had already taken her to the far-flung corners of the earth. Would it be so bad to stay in one place?

Not if it was the right place.

As she hung up the phone, she realized that the right place for her had nothing to do with a physical location. The right place would be where she could make a home and a life with Brian.

Were his feelings as strong? She simply wasn't sure. He liked her, she could tell that, but his guilt over his wife's death had a strong hold on his heart. She prayed she could help him find the forgiveness he needed.

Over the next week, Brian managed to make time to see Lindsey almost every day. One night they enjoyed quiet conversation over a delectable dinner at a small romantic café. On New Year's Eve, he joined both Lindsey and Karen for dinner at their apartment. Lindsey freely gave Karen credit for the hearty cooking he sampled. While the sisters laughed together over stories of previous cooking failures, he was free to admire how beautiful Lindsey's face looked when she was happy and carefree.

The following Friday night he took her to see the latest blockbuster action movie. The place was nearly empty with most of the students gone for the holiday break. Holding Lindsey's hand in a dark theater, he paid little attention to the story unfolding on the screen. What he saw was a new chapter unfolding in his own life and he liked what he saw. He knew it was too soon to talk about marriage, but the idea took hold in the back of his mind and wouldn't leave.

When he took her home that evening, they stood for a short while on her front porch and shared another sweet kiss full of promise and hope. Unbidden, the words, "I love you," rose from his heart and crossed his lips.

Her luminous eyes widened and filled with joy. "Oh, Brian, I love you, too."

"I could stand to hear those words every day of my life."

"It would be easy to say them every day," she said with quiet sincerity.

He wanted to say more, but found he didn't yet have the courage. For now, it was enough to know that she loved him. In time, they would talk about what the future might hold for them together.

On Saturday morning, Brian was determined to enjoy a few quiet hours at home after his evening with Lindsey. The trouble was, he couldn't stop thinking about her. In the light of day, it all seemed unreal. Had she really said that she loved him? Could they have a future together? The new year seemed to hold so much promise. Just thinking about it scared him witless.

All he wanted to do was to be with Lindsey. He wanted to see her eyes light up when they met his. He wanted to hold her in his arms and kiss her soft lips. He wanted to feel this happy every day of his life.

Their evening at the Bible-study class had given him a lot of food for thought. He wasn't certain that he was willing to accept Lindsey's version of a loving and caring God, but he was willing to listen and learn more from the energetic young pastor he had met.

Deciding it was better to work than to moon over a woman, he took out his seminar speech and began practicing it aloud. An hour later, Isabella went scampering through the living room past his chair toward the front entrance. She slid into the door panel then began to hop up and down.

He listened carefully and heard the faint clank of the mailbox closing. Limping to the door, he scooped up the excited rabbit and held on to her as he opened the door and fetched his mail. The grocery store flyers were exactly the kind of paper Isabella delighted in shredding. Back inside the house, he closed the door firmly before putting her down. Her recent escapes at work had made him much more cautious about keeping an eye on her.

Once she was on the floor, she darted to her special box, hopped in and then stood on her hind legs to peer at him over the rim. Her anticipation was obvious.

Sitting in his recliner, he quickly tossed the discount ads in with her. As the crackle and ripping of paper replaced the quiet of the house, he grinned and began to look through the rest of his mail. A small, pale blue envelope caught his attention. A painful spasm clenched his stomach when he read the return address. He glanced at his wife's face in the photo on the table beside him.

"It's from your mother."

His in-laws had spoken to him only once after Emily's death. Three days after the accident, his father-in-law had come to Brian's hospital room to tell him they had arranged to have the funeral in their hometown sixty miles away the following day. Groggy from pain medication and still in traction for his shattered hip, Brian had begged him to wait until he could attend, but Emily's father had walked out of the room without saying anything else.

No words could have conveyed more strongly the blame they placed on Brian for their beloved daughter's death. He tried phoning, but they never took his calls. The few letters he wrote came back unopened. Now, after all this time, the note in his hand was the first contact he'd had from them.

Irritation battled with his curiosity. He had loved Emily and she had loved him. If her parents had offered even the slightest sign of forgiveness, perhaps he could have found a way to forgive himself, too.

He held the unopened letter over Isabella's box, but he didn't drop it. Instead, he tore open the envelope and pulled out a single sheet of pale blue stationary.

Brian,

This coming February will mark the fifth anniversary of Emily's death, as I'm sure you are aware. Her father and I have planned a memorial service for the occasion. As the passing years have dulled our grief, we have come to regret the way we excluded you from our lives.

You were Emily's one true love and we know that you never meant to hurt her. Our excuse is that our lives ended with the death of our only child. Our grief and anger needed an outlet and it was easy to blame you.

I hope you will accept our invitation to attend her memorial service. Perhaps in this way we can begin to make amends for the way we treated you. Please join us as our family and friends come together to celebrate Emily's life.

Grace and Emit Todd

Tears blurred his vision as he glanced to his wife's face smiling at him from the silver frame. She would be happy to know her parents were making an attempt to repair their relationship with him. Noticing a thin coat of dust on the glass, he realized that he hadn't held her picture close in weeks. Guilt cut deep in his heart.

He picked up the photo and wiped the front with his sleeve then pressed it to his chest. "I've been forgetting you. How could I do that? I'm sorry, sweetheart. I'm sorry about everything."

It was because of Lindsey. Lindsey had turned his life upside down and made him dream about happiness again. How could he be happy when he had ruined the lives of so many people? Her life, their child's life. Her parents were suffering still. What right did he have to any happiness in the face of so much sorrow?

The clock on the wall chimed twelve times. Today was his day to volunteer at Hearts and Horses. He was scheduled to be there at two o'clock. For a second, he considered calling to say he couldn't make it, but that would only place more of a burden on his friend. He would go, but first he would answer the letter from Emily's parents and tell them he would join them in February.

Later in the afternoon, Brian stepped out of his truck in front of the Hearts and Horses stable. He turned up the collar of his black overcoat against the chilling wind, then pulled his cane out from behind the front seat. As he made his way across the gravel driveway to the office door beside the barn, he glanced around at the well-groomed farm.

White rail fences bordered the road and enclosed several corrals. The old two-story house was also painted white, but bright blue shutters kept it from looking austere. An American flag fluttered in the breeze from its holder on one of the porch's tall square columns. In the spring and summer, Brian knew the green lawns were bordered with colorful flower beds, but winter had put an end to their bright displays weeks ago.

He stopped at the office door, but Patience Duncan opened it before he had a chance to knock. Patience's erect bearing and boundless energy belied her sixty-odd years. Her salt-and-pepper gray hair was cut in a simple bob. Her worn jeans were tucked into tall black rubber boots and her green hooded parka had a hole in one elbow where an occasional down feather found its way to freedom.

"Brian, thank you for coming." She threw her arms around him in a hearty hug.

"I'm always happy to help." He was glad now that he had come. He needed to get away from his somber thoughts.

Patience stepped back. "Come in out of the wind. It sure turned cold fast. Makes me doubly glad our indoor arena is finished."

Brian followed her inside the office. A second door connected the cluttered room to the larger pole barn. "Are my pupils here yet?"

"I'm only expecting one child today. The boy you referred to us."

"Mark? Is this his first time?"

"It is. He was disappointed when I told him he wouldn't actually be riding today, just getting to know Sprite and learning to take of her. His mother seemed very relieved. I think she needs this therapy more than her son does."

"You may be right."

"I'm happy for the light schedule because the army is sending out one of their horses for evaluation today."

His heart sank. The last thing he wanted to do was face Lindsey today. Perhaps she wouldn't be one of the people who brought Tiger. He could only hope. "I've seen the horse in action. I think he'll be great for you."

"I hope so. Speaking of the army, I think that must be them." Patience stepped to the office window and drew the blue-and-white-checked curtain aside.

Brian moved to stand beside her. The red pickup and matching red trailer rumbling into the circle driveway were unmistakable. His heart jumped into overdrive when he noticed Lindsey in the front seat between Avery and Shane.

Patience let the curtain fall back into place. "Why don't you show them where to take their horse."

"Mark and his mother are waiting. I should get started with them."

"All right. I've set up the arena so that you can have the back third. I'll go meet the troops." Patience gave him an odd look as she walked past.

Lindsey had noticed Brian's truck in the driveway as soon as they pulled in. Excitement and delight raced through her, leaving her giddy with joy.

Resisting the urge to run and find him and fling herself into his arms took a fair measure of her resolve. There would be time for that later. Today, she was under orders to assess this facility as a possible home for a valued member of their unit. She didn't take her assignment lightly.

A middle-aged woman came out of the office and walked toward them. "Hello, and welcome to Hearts and Horses. Call me Patience. You'll never meet anyone so misnamed." The woman flashed a broad friendly smile that put Lindsey instantly at ease.

"Good afternoon, ma'am. I'm Sergeant Mandel and this is Corporal Ross and Private Barnes."

"It's a pleasure to meet you. Well, let's get a look at your horse, shall we?" Patience strode to the rear of the trailer without waiting for anyone. "How old did you say he was?" she called over her shoulder.

"Eighteen," Shane answered as he hurried to keep up with her.

"A good age for horses and for men. How old are you, sonny?"

Lindsey smiled at Avery. "I like her already."

A clang signaled the rear gate of the trailer opening. Lindsey and Avery followed as Shane and Patience led Tiger into the barn. Across the arena, Lindsey saw Brian introducing Mark to a small black mare with two white stockings and a star on her forehead. Mark's grin told Lindsey exactly what he thought of his new friend. When Brian looked their way, Lindsey smiled and waved. He nodded in acknowledgment, but continued to give his attention to the boy. Puzzled by his less-than-enthusiastic greeting, she worried that she had done something to upset him. The idea was ridiculous. He had seemed fine when they parted company last night, but she couldn't shake the feeling that something was wrong.

Patience quickly began a series of tests for Tiger. First, she rode him bareback around a small section of the barn to get the animal used to her and his surroundings. Next, she asked Shane to walk him on a loose lead and guide him beside a long ramp. Once alongside the platform, Patience turned around backward and had Shane continue to lead the horse while she shifted her weight numerous times. It was obvious that Tiger was surprised by the activity, but he remained calm and composed. Patience dismounted and pushed a wheelchair up to Tiger. He sniffed it over, then proceeded to ignore it as she pushed it close beside him, even bumping into him slightly.

While Tiger and the men got a workout with Patience, Lindsey had time to watch Brian's interaction with Mark and the horse. His quiet confidence and gentle encouragement soon had the boy and his mother brushing the mare's coat and feeding her treats. A few minutes later, Brian took them over to show them the special saddle Mark would be using. It was fastened to a stand with handrails around it and Brian had Mark practice transferring on and off until he seemed satisfied the boy could do it without difficulty.

After a half hour, Mark and his mother left. Brian began walking toward the door just as Patience declared an end to her test. She told Shane to tie up Tiger and follow her. Dusting off her hands, she came to stand beside Lindsey. "I think he's a keeper. He's cool, calm and collected and he seems readily adaptable. That's exactly the kind of horse we need. My thanks to the army for thinking of us."

"It was Brian's idea." Lindsey was happy to give him credit.

"Then my thanks to you, Brian," Patience called out. He stopped as the group led by Patience closed the distance between them.

"I have tea and coffee in the office and a dozen oatmeal cookies that I don't want going to my waist — so you are instructed to go in and enjoy them. Let me put Sprite up and then I'll give you the grand tour afterward so you can see if my stable meets your requirements. No arguments. Brian, show them the way."

"I really should be going."

"Nonsense. I've never known you to pass up one of my cookies. What's wrong with you?"

"Nothing's wrong with me," he said defensively.

"Well, then, go show my guests a little hospitality until I get back," she muttered as she tromped off.

Lindsey studied Brian, but he wouldn't look at her. Something was definitely wrong.

Avery settled his cap more tightly on his

head. "Nobody has to tell me twice to eat oatmeal cookies."

They all began walking toward the office. "She would have done well in the military," Shane said as he held open the door for the others.

"She certainly enjoys giving orders," Avery agreed.

Shane patted Brian on the shoulder. "I've found most women do, especially women sergeants. Have you sent in your reenlistment papers yet, Lindsey?"

"They're filled out, but I haven't turned them in."

"You're still planning to reenlist?" Brian asked, a scowl on his face as he looked at her for the first time.

The disapproval in his tone cut her to the quick. "Brian, the army is my career."

He glared at her. "I thought things had changed."

"Have they? I don't recall being asked anything except to consider it."

Shane cleared his throat. "I'm going to go load Tiger. Avery, come help me." He grabbed two cookies and pushed Avery toward the door back into the barn.

Lindsey crossed her arms over her chest. "I thought you understood my feelings."

"Yes, you always made them clear."

"I hope I have." She couldn't help the defensive tone in her voice. "I plan to ask for an assignment at Fort Riley."

"But you can't guarantee they'll give you that assignment, can you?"

"Of course not."

"For you it's the army, your country, your family, your horse and then Lindsey somewhere way at the back of the line."

"Brian, what's wrong? Why are you so angry?"

"I thought we had something good between us."

"I thought so, too."

"Then where do I fit in your list, Lindsey? After the army but before the horse?"

"That's not fair." The hurt his tone caused went deeper than she had ever imagined.

"Life isn't fair and you didn't answer my question."

"How can I give you an answer when we've never talked about it?"

Shaking his head, he walked to the door and pulled it open. "The same way you made your decision to reenlist without talking to me about it."

He slammed the door behind him, leaving her staring after him with no idea what had just happened.

CHAPTER THIRTEEN

Lindsey tried to pretend that everything was okay. She went to work and to her physical therapy sessions, but her arm seemed to be getting weaker instead of stronger. She spent long hours walking Dakota, first around the small pen beside the stable and later on longer trips through the pastures and along the less traveled roads of the base. When it was only the big horse walking beside her, she didn't have to pretend, and the tears that she tried to hold in check would slip out.

Shane, Avery and Lee offered a few times to go with her, but she politely refused. After a few days they seemed to realize that solitude was exactly what she wanted and needed. Captain Watson made sure that the unit ran smoothly as preparations got underway for their trip to Washington, D.C. All the horses were outfitted with the special shoes that were required, uniforms were pressed and boots were buffed to a high gloss. Lindsey went through the motions without thinking about them.

When the first heavy snowfall blanketed the base, she tried not to remember how happy she had been with Brian in the snow on Christmas night. Her heart might be broken, but it would heal in time the way her arm and Dakota's leg had healed. Breaks were excruciatingly painful in the beginning, but with time the pain would fade to a dull ache. If she could just find a way to get through it until then.

When anyone asked about Brian, she would smile and say he was too busy to come out to the base. She thought she had convinced the rest of the unit that she was fine. It was her sister she couldn't fool.

A week after the trip to Hearts and Horses, Karen confronted Lindsey in the kitchen of their apartment.

"All right. What is going on?" Karen demanded, standing in the doorway with her hands propped on her hips.

"I'm not sure I know what you mean. I'm setting the table for dinner."

"You know exactly what I mean. What happened between you and Brian?"

"Nothing happened." She lined up the spoons beside the knives.

"One night you float in here telling me how in love you are and the next night I hear you crying yourself to sleep. Okay, call me crazy, but I think something is going on."

"It didn't work out. What do you want me to say?"

"A little more than that."

Stepping up to her sister, Lindsey laid her hand on Karen's shoulder. "It didn't work out. That's all there is to it. Now can we please talk about something else?"

"Do I need to have Shane go punch his lights out?"

Lindsey managed a weak smile. "As satisfying as that may sound, it won't help."

"I didn't think so. Oh, honey, I'm so sorry."

"Thanks, but it's better to find out now than after we've spent seventeen years together the way Mom and Dad did."

"I think it's better to fall in love and stay in love."

"That isn't the path God has chosen for me."

"You shouldn't give up so easily. You love the guy. Take my advice and go talk to him. Isn't he worth fighting for?"

He was, but she didn't know how or who to fight. Brian had made the choice to end their relationship before it truly began. She strongly suspected his motives had more to do with his guilt over his wife's death than her career choice, but she didn't know how to make him see that. Tonight, she was too tired to search for answers.

"I've got a more important battle to win. I have to get Dakota fit to go to the Inauguration. I'm not going to disappoint Danny when he has worked so hard. After Washington, D.C., maybe I'll go and see Brian. Until then, can we please not talk about him anymore?"

Karen reluctantly agreed and Lindsey was almost sorry she did.

Lindsey threw a saddle up on Dakota for the first time since their fall. It proved to be difficult with her weak arm, but she managed. It had been three weeks since his cast had come off. He was up to walking five miles a day without problems. To her eye, he looked as sound as a dollar, but the real test would be to see if he could carry her weight.

The company horses were due to depart for Washington, D.C., in two days. The decision whether or not to take Dakota had to made within the next forty-eight hours.

In the small enclosed riding pen beside

the stable, she spoke softly to him and stepped into the stirrup. He stood motionless as she swung up onto his back.

"Good boy. Let's try a walk, okay?" She nudged him with her heels and he began walking with a smooth stride that gladdened her heart.

After ten circuits of the area without any sign of lameness, she pulled him to a halt.

"How does he feel, Sergeant?" Captain Watson asked from the stable doorway.

"As good as he looks, sir." She patted Dakota's neck.

"Excellent. All we need now is Dr. Cutter's okay and Dakota is on his way with the rest of the herd."

Just the mention of Brian's name was enough to make her want to cry, but she didn't give in to the urge. Once more she'd had it pounded into her head that a military life and romance didn't mix. This time she had learned her lesson for good.

"I don't see any reason Dr. Cutter won't release him. His walk is sound."

Captain Watson stepped out of the stable and came to stand beside her. Under one arm he carried the unit's banner.

Lindsey's heart sank. Her grip wasn't strong in spite of the physical therapy that she had been doing religiously.

"Are you ready to try this?" he asked, nodding toward the staff in his hand.

"Yes, sir." Lindsey was happy her voice sounded calm even if she was quaking inside.

Please, dear Lord. I need Your help now. Lend me the strength I need to do this for my brother.

Captain Watson handed up the banner. As soon as her fingers closed around the staff, she knew she couldn't hold it. The flag slipped out of her grasp. He caught it before it hit the ground.

He didn't say anything. He didn't have to. She dismounted and spent a long moment staring at her boots before she looked up and met his sympathetic gaze. The choking pain in her chest made it almost impossible to speak, but she did. "I respectfully request that you appoint another soldier to carry the flag, sir."

"Lindsey, I'm sorry."

"Don't be sorry. It never was about me. It's about honoring men and women like Danny — people who have given everything, including their lives, to protect and defend our flag. The last thing I want to do is disrespect their sacrifice by dropping the colors."

"Do you feel that you can hold a saber in salute?"

Oh, how she wanted to say she could, but the truth came out instead. "I doubt it."

"I see."

"Does this mean that I'll stay behind as part of the rear detachment?"

"No. Your family will be there and so should you. As you know, normally flag bearing goes by rank."

"Yes, sir. Highest-ranking soldier carries the U.S. flag, next highest rank carries the army flag and so on."

"That means Corporal Ross will carry the American flag in your place."

"Sir, my concern is that Shane's weight will be too much for Dakota."

"I agree. I'll leave it to you to decide who will ride Dakota in your place. At least he will be in the parade to represent your family if Dr. Cutter okays the trip."

"Yes, sir. I know Danny will be honored to have any one of our unit members ride Dakota."

"Thank you, Sergeant. You're dismissed for the day. Let me know who your choice is tomorrow morning."

Trying hard to maintain control, Lindsey saluted smartly, then watched the Captain walk away. When he was out of sight, she buried her face in Dakota's mane and gave in to her tears.

Brian pulled up the most recent digital X-rays of Dakota's leg on the computer in his office. They weren't the best-quality films. The fourth-year students he had sent to the base to take the X-rays that morning hadn't done as good a job as he would have liked. He should have gone himself, but he hadn't wanted to risk running into Lindsey.

He leaned forward to examine the pictures more closely. He couldn't be sure if the faint line extending into the second phalanx bone was artifact or new trouble brewing for Dakota.

He looked up at the sound of a knock on his door. Jennifer opened it and said, "Doctor, Captain Watson and Sergeant Mandel are here to see you."

His heart sank. So much for avoiding Lindsey. He steeled his heart against the pain he knew was coming. "Send them in."

He rose and extended his hand as Captain Watson entered. The Captain took it in a firm grip. Lindsey came in and stood quietly behind her commander.

"We've come to get a travel release for Dakota."

"I'm afraid I have some concerns about that."

Captain Watson frowned. "What type of concerns?"

"His last X-ray shows a small area that has me worried. I'd like to repeat the films tomorrow."

"I'm sorry, Doctor, but the horses are due to ship out tomorrow morning and my men will be flying out the following afternoon. The custom hauler the army has hired will be at the stable at ten sharp. If you need more films you'll have to get them today."

"You're using a custom hauler? I thought your men would be taking the horses."

"Army regulations make that difficult. If we haul the horses ourselves, we would have to stop every eight hours and rest the animals. The trip would take days. By hiring an outside firm, the horses can be transported straight through to Washington, D.C."

Brian frowned. "You're talking about almost twenty-four hours without a break."

"That's correct."

"I'm afraid I can't release Dakota to travel under such conditions."

"Why not?" Lindsey demanded, looking at him for the first time.

"Standing in a moving trailer and being

jostled in amongst other animals for so many hours would place entirely too much stress on his leg. I'm sorry, but I won't grant his release under such circumstances."

Captain Watson glanced at Lindsey. "I'm certainly disappointed to hear that. This is a very important event for my men. They've worked hard to get Dakota fit and ready to go."

"I understand that, but the risk to the animal's welfare is simply too great."

"I can't take the horse without a release." He looked back and forth between Brian and Lindsey as if waiting for more to be said. When neither of them spoke, he drew a deep breath. "That's it then. Thank you for your time, Dr. Cutter."

Lindsey waited until Captain Watson left the room. When he closed the door behind him, she swung around to face Brian. "How can you do this to me? You know how important this is!"

"I'm not doing anything *to* you. I'm doing this *for* Dakota."

Lindsey stared at Brian in growing disbelief. "He's healed."

"And I intend to see that he stays that way."

"Brian, you know how important it is that he be in the parade, how important it is to my brother."

"I know you want Dakota there to honor your brother, but what good will it do if Dakota's leg fails on the trailer ride and he has to be destroyed? I know you don't want that."

"He can make the trip. He's strong enough."

"Maybe he is and maybe he isn't. As his vet, this is my call. I can't let you risk his life for a few minutes of fame."

"You mean you won't risk letting the world see that your wonderful new procedure doesn't work." Disappointment gave her words a bitter edge.

"It did work. Dakota was out of his cast in record time."

"But his leg isn't strong enough to stand the trip to Washington, D.C.? How is that a success? Why not let us at least try using a sling or some way to support him?"

"I might agree to that if I knew the trip could be made in easy stages, but you heard Captain Watson. The horses are going nonstop by commercial hauler. That means hours of being shaken and jarred and crowded in with fifteen other animals. The risk is too much. Especially after all it took to save him in the first place."

"But to not even try?"

"You're upset. I don't think this discussion needs to go any further."

"I thought you understood what was at stake. My brother is going to be at that parade. How am I going to tell him Dakota won't be?"

"Lindsey, I'm sorry."

"I wanted to carry the flag for him, but I can't. My arm isn't strong enough. So, I want Dakota there because he was an important part of Danny's life. When my brother gave Dakota to the army, it was his last piece of freedom, his last ounce of pride. He had nothing left to give his country and now you're going to say that sacrifice means nothing."

"Do you honestly think your brother would want you to risk Dakota's life?"

At his question, the fight went out of Lindsey. "No."

He stepped close. If only he would take her in his arms the way he had before. How could the feelings between them have changed so quickly?

"Go to Washington, D.C., Lindsey. Ride beside the flag with your unit. Honor your brother's sacrifice, even if it isn't in the fashion you had hoped."

She pulled away from his touch. "I want to thank you for all you have done for

Dakota, Dr. Cutter. You have the gratitude of the U.S. Army. I can see myself out."

As she walked out the door of his office, Brian knew with a sinking heart that she was walking out of his life.

He started to go after her, but stopped with his hand on the doorknob. It was for the best. He didn't have a heart to give her. He had buried it with his wife and child.

If I don't have a heart, then what is breaking inside me?

CHAPTER FOURTEEN

Work had always been Brian's answer to keeping his innermost pain locked away. Today should have been no different, except nothing helped erase the memory of the disappointment on Lindsey's face when she had walked out of his office two days ago.

He glanced at the clock above his desk. It was only a few minutes after nine. The unit's horses would be almost to Washington, D.C., by now. Except for Dakota. Lindsey and the other soldiers would be flying out in a few hours. The Inaugural parade would take place tomorrow at noon.

"And my conference is less than forty-eight hours away," he muttered.

What he needed now was to concentrate on his presentation, to make sure he had enough hard facts to impress the United Jockey Club representatives and ensure substantial grant monies for his research. He needed to focus. Reaching for a pencil, he paused with it in his hand. The memory of Lindsey grinning at him with one between her teeth made him smile. Remembering the kiss he had shared with her in this office erased all thoughts of work from him mind.

"You're a fool, Brian Cutter," he stated forcefully. "What right did you have to fall in love again?"

It was a question to which he already knew the answer. He had no right to love another woman. His carelessness had cost Emily her life. She had loved him with all her heart and trusted him to care for her always. He never should have survived the crash. He should have died with her and the baby.

Passing through what was left of his days without love had seemed a fitting punishment for living. Until Lindsey.

Lindsey had made him think about a future and not about the past.

He heard a timid knock at the door. An irrational hope rose that it might be her, but it was quickly dashed when Jennifer peeked in.

"I thought I made it plain that I didn't want to be disturbed." He turned away before she could read the disappointment he knew must be written on his face.

"Someone is in a sour mood today."

"What do you want?"

"Wow, the list is so long. A new car, a diamond tennis bracelet, a trip to Jamaica . . ."

"If you think you can get all of those things with your first unemployment check, keep making jokes."

The sudden silence told him he had made his point. After a moment, she cleared her throat and said meekly, "I wanted to inform you that your ambulance has arrived."

"Thank you, I've been informed. Is that all?" When she didn't reply, he turned around. She was standing in the doorway tapping her cheek with one finger as she stared at the ceiling. She sighed as if she had come to an important decision.

"The unemployment check might make a down payment on the tennis bracelet, so I'm going to go ahead and tell you that you are an abject idiot."

The last thing he needed was one of her scoldings. "Jen, please. Not today."

"You let your friend down. Even if there was nothing romantic between you and Lindsey, and I don't believe that for a minute, but even if there wasn't, she was your friend."

"I had no way of proving that Dakota's

leg would be strong enough for the journey."

"You mean you don't have enough data to make that assumption."

He threw his hands up. "Exactly. Finally, someone understands."

"But you believe in your work, don't you?"

"Of course I do. Dakota will be as sound as ever."

She crossed her arms and asked, "How much proof would you need?"

"I don't understand."

"How much proof of his soundness would you need to let him go to Washington?"

"Perhaps another month without any signs of lameness."

"Was he sound before?"

"Before the accident? I assume so."

"He was sound and he broke his pastern anyway."

"Jennifer, what are you getting at?"

She stepped forward and laid a hand on his arm. "What I'm getting at is that we never get a guarantee in life. All we get are opportunities. In life and in love there are no guarantees. We get hurt, we lose, we cry and then we get up and keep going because God made us this way. The only guarantee of failure is in not trying."

Why did what she was saying suddenly make so much sense?

She crossed her arms over her chest again and stared at him. Arching one eyebrow, she asked, "So, am I fired?"

Her cheeky question pulled a wry smile from him. "I'll let you know by the end of the day."

"I'd like to know now. Stylish Gems jewelry shop is having a sale. My bracelet is twenty percent off if I put it on layaway by noon."

"You aren't fired."

She sighed. "It's just as well. I never learned to play tennis. Okay, come outside and show me your new toy."

It beat trying to work surrounded by memories he couldn't forget. The horses had already left. Even if he did change his decision it wouldn't change the outcome for Dakota. Grabbing his cane, he accompanied Jennifer out the main doors.

In the parking lot beside the clinic, the equine ambulance sat looking like a white, overly tall and extra-wide horse trailer.

"This is it? This is what you've been begging for?" Jennifer didn't look impressed.

"Don't let its unassuming exterior fool you. This is the best they make." Brian had spent long hours poring over the features of this particular model. He pressed a switch on the front. A muffled hiss filled the air as the hydraulic system allowed the entire trailer to sink to ground level.

A second switch lowered one whole wall of the vehicle and turned it into a gentle ramp. "This will keep an injured horse from having to step up."

"Cool." Apparently intrigued, she ventured closer. "What's that?" She pointed inside.

"Those are hydraulic padded sides that move in and hold the animal still so he doesn't have to shift his weight. There is a sling, too, if one is needed, and a winch to pull the horse in if it can't stand."

"So a horse could ride in this thing and never put a hoof on the floor?"

"I guess that's true."

"If the army had something like this, then Dakota could travel to Washington, D.C., and not risk injuring his leg."

"The Army doesn't have anything like this, believe me."

"No, because we have it. For how long?"

"Two weeks."

She patted his shoulder. "I knew you'd think of something."

He followed her sudden shift in logic way too easily. "No. No! I'm not giving this vehicle to the army."

"Loan, not give. Loan for a few days.

Calm down."

He rubbed his chin as he considered what she was suggesting. It was crazy. Unthinkable. "The unit is leaving today. There isn't time to get over there."

"Avery said they aren't leaving until noon. It's only ten-thirty. You've got plenty of time."

"This is insane. They wouldn't even know how to operate it."

"You know how."

"Me? I can't go to Washington, D.C. I've got to present a lecture at the conference the day after tomorrow."

"What will you lose by missing one lecture?"

"Funding, respect, a chance to prove my work is making a difference."

"Fair enough. What will you gain by missing it?"

What would he gain? A chance to make things right with Lindsey? A chance to make amends for his cruel behavior? A chance to let a brave man see that his sacrifice meant something to this nation?

He turned to walk away. "No. I'll get fired."

She raced to stand in front of him, blocking his retreat. "You have tenure. They won't fire you."

He stepped to the side, but she moved to match him. "I'll end up teaching the first year's bone lab."

"So what? You'll be great at it."

He shook his head. "No, I can't do it."

"Dr. Cutter, look at me." When he did, she said quietly. "Tell me that you don't love her."

The words couldn't come out of his mouth, because he knew they weren't true. He did love Lindsey. He would always love her. God had blessed him and he had turned his back on that blessing. He had been too scared of coming alive again, of risking more heartache, and because of that he had pushed Lindsey away. Would this wild scheme give him another chance? Or was it already too late?

Like a gentle whisper in his ear, he heard Lindsey's voice saying, "We use our head to make a lot of decisions in life, but some decisions have to be made with the heart. This is one of them. Do what your heart tells you is right."

Lord, I know it's been a long time since You've heard a prayer from me, but please let this be the right decision.

Lindsey stood apart from the rest of the unit as they waited beside the barn for the bus that would take them to the airport. She didn't want to dampen the excitement of the others. Attired in their sharply pressed dress uniforms, the men were laughing and joking and bursting with pride. This was the most prestigious event many of them would ever attend in their entire lives. Tomorrow, families from across the nation would be glued to their televisions hoping for a glimpse of their sons, grandsons or fathers as this unit rode proudly down Pennsylvania Avenue — without her.

Lindsey blew on her hands and wished she hadn't packed her gloves away. The air was cold and crisp enough to frost the windows of the office with lacy patterns. Karen sat beside her on an overstuffed suitcase bundled up to her ears with a thick red-white-and-blue scarf over her heavy quilted blue parka. The Captain had managed to secure a seat for her on the military flight and for that Lindsey was grateful. When the bus rolled into sight at last, Lindsey said, "I'm just going to run in and say goodbye to Dakota. I know he wonders why he was left behind."

Karen pulled down her scarf enough to say, "I won't let them leave without you."

"I almost wish they would."

"No, you don't. Danny, Abigail and Dad

all want to see you."

"I let them down. I let Danny down."

"Did he take it badly when you called last night?"

"It almost broke my heart to tell him that Dakota and I were going to have to sit this one out." Her heart was already in so many pieces that Lindsey wondered if it would ever be whole again.

"I'm sure he understands that it wasn't your fault."

"He tried to be cheerful and upbeat, but I could tell he was so disappointed."

"Our brother is a strong guy."

"He is. He tried to make me feel better by telling me he was glad he didn't have to get out in the cold tomorrow. I let him down. I don't know how I'm going to face him."

"You did your best. You can feel sorry for yourself all you want, but your family still loves you, so get over it." She covered her nose again.

Lindsey couldn't help but smile. "When we were little I used to ask God over and over again why He gave me such a pain in the neck for a sister. Little did I know what a favor He did me and how much I would come to cherish you."

"What a sweet thing to say. But for the record, I thought you were a pain in the neck, too," came her muffled reply.

Lindsey's giggles mingled with her sister's. It felt good to laugh again.

The bus pulled into the parking lot, but a second vehicle pulled in behind it. Lindsey looked on in amazement as Brian got out of his truck and started toward her. The laughter and voices of the men grew silent as they watched him approach. Shane, Lee and Avery stepped in front of her, blocking Brian's way.

Facing the men with their arms crossed over their chests and scowls on their faces, Brian knew it wouldn't be easy to persuade Lindsey's friends to let him speak to her.

Captain Watson stepped out in front of the group. "Dr. Cutter, what brings you here today?"

Brian decided his best chance would be to make this offer seem professional instead of personal. "I've come to put a proposal to you, Captain."

"What type of proposal?"

"I'd like to transport Dakota to Washington for you."

He saw Lindsey's eyes widen in surprise. A murmur ran through the group until the Captain held up his hand for silence. "I don't think I understand. You said it wouldn't be safe for him to make such a long trailer ride."

"I now have a special ambulance that can transport Dakota in complete safety without placing any undue stress on his leg. I'm willing to take him if I can have another man go with me to share the driving."

Lindsey spoke at last. "I thought the ambulance was going to be on display for the conference. How did you get permission to take it across the country?"

Since he didn't exactly have permission, he chose his words carefully. "The vehicle is on loan to the clinic for two weeks. There is no stipulation that it stays in our parking lot. In fact, we especially asked that we be allowed to use it for patient transports." He shrugged. "No mention was made about how far those transports might be."

He watched as the possibility of seeing her dream come true brightened her eyes, replacing the coolness she had regarded him with. He hoped she could read the regret on his face as easily as he read her growing excitement.

The Captain looked at his watch. "You would be cutting it close to make D.C. by assembly time tomorrow."

"I know that."

"I wouldn't feel right sending one of my

men with you knowing they might miss riding in the parade."

Lindsey stepped between her friends and addressed Captain Watson. "Sir, I respectfully request that I be allowed to accompany Dakota since I won't be riding."

"Me, too," Karen added, wiggling between Shane and Lee.

Captain Watson rubbed a hand over his jaw. "This is highly irregular, but I do have orders for *all* our horses to travel to Washington, D.C., by independent contactor."

Karen looked around. "Does that mean he can go?"

"Corporal Ross," the Captain barked.

"Sir." Shane stepped forward.

"Get the forge fired up and get those special shoes on Dakota."

"Yes, sir." He replied with a bright grin.

Karen's shriek of joy was echoed in Brian's heart. Now he would have twenty-four hours to try to set things right with Lindsey.

With the help of all the unit members, they soon had Dakota shod and secured in the trailer along with enough feed and water to last the trip. Lindsey and Karen stowed their suitcases behind the seat of the truck and then came to stand beside Brian.

He said, "There's a jump seat in the trailer. One of us should ride back here and

279

keep an eye on him. There's a walkie-talkie by the seat and one in the truck cab so we can keep in touch."

"I'll ride with him," Lindsey said, and moved to climb in.

Karen caught her by the arm. "Oh, no you don't. I'm taking the first turn with Dakota." She pushed past her sister to stand in the open doorway at the rear of the trailer.

Brian could have kissed her. He walked to the front of the truck and waited beside the passenger door.

"Karen, you're riding in the truck and that's an order." Lindsey's low tone brooked no argument.

"I'm not in the military. I don't take orders. Stop being a coward and go get in the truck or we'll never get there."

Lindsey considered jerking her sister out of the trailer, but decided she didn't want to look that undignified in front of her men. Instead, she slammed the rear door shut, walked up beside Brian and climbed into the cab.

Moments later, he got in behind the wheel, started the engine and pulled out onto the road. Long minutes passed as they drove through the base on the winding, narrow road. She didn't say anything and neither did he.

It wasn't until he pulled out onto Interstate 70 fifteen minutes later that she gave in and spoke first.

"I thought your big conference was the day after tomorrow?"

"It is."

"You'll never make it back from D.C. unless you plan to fly."

"I can't fly. I have to drive this trailer back."

She looked at him in surprise. "What about your presentation? What about the bigwigs with money who will fund your research if you wow them?"

"They won't be wowed by me. Hopefully, my research will speak for itself when I publish the study later on."

Lindsey couldn't quite get her mind around the idea that he had given up a chance for peer recognition and substantial additional funding . . . for her. A slim thread of hope began to bind up the shattered pieces of her heart. "Why are you doing this?"

He looked over at her. "Because my head said this was a crazy idea, but my heart said it was the right thing to do."

His eyes, so intense and full of sincerity, begged her to believe him. A whirlwind of emotions swirled through her mind. "I don't know what to say."

"Then let me start by saying I'm sorry that I treated you so badly that day at Hearts and Horses. I know I have some explaining to do."

She settled back in the seat and crossed her arms over her chest. "Yes, you do."

"Until I met you, I had kept the pain of my wife's death very much alive. The accident was my fault and I wanted — no, I needed — some kind of punishment for being the one to live."

"Survivor's guilt."

"Is that what they call it?"

"Yes. That still doesn't explain why you were so angry about my reenlistment."

"I wasn't angry about that. I was angry because I had allowed myself to fall in love with you. Your reenlistment was just an excuse to push you away. I would have found some other reason to stop seeing you. I didn't believe that I deserved to be loved."

She wasn't sure she was ready to accept what he had to say at face value.

"You really hurt me."

"What can I do to make you forgive me?"

"Groveling might be good," she suggested.

He managed a small smile. "I'll do that the first chance I get."

"Telling the truth is always a winner, too."

"All right, the truth. I have been afraid since the first moment I saw you."

"Afraid of what?"

"Of living and loving and perhaps losing that love. I couldn't face those risks, but I couldn't forget about you, either, and that scared me witless."

"All of life is a risk, Brian. Only God knows what lies in store for us."

"I'm trying to accept that, but it's hard to have faith in something I can't see or touch."

She reached across and laid her hand on his arm. "You can't see or touch love, yet you still believe in it, don't you?"

"Yes, I do believe love exists."

"Then so does God. God *is* love."

"Is it really that simple?"

"It really is."

"Have I told you how beautiful and wise you are?"

"No, but I may allow you to do so for the next thousand miles."

He chuckled, but quickly sobered. He took one hand off the wheel to clasp hers tightly. "Lindsey, I need to know that I haven't ruined what we had between us."

Her hand felt so small and snug in his grip. When she was eighty years old, would she still want to hold this man's hand? "My feelings for you haven't changed, Brian. I don't expect that they ever will."

"If I wasn't driving seventy miles an hour I would kiss you, darling. I love you so much it hurts."

"I love you, too, and we're going to have to stop for gas sometime."

He laughed out loud and squeezed her hand. "I promise to make up for lost time at our first pit stop. Sergeant Lindsey Mandel, will you marry me?"

In the sudden and telling silence, Brian glanced at Lindsey in concern. A second later his newfound bubble of happiness nose-dived toward the floor. "What? What's wrong?"

"Oh, talk about being scared. Brian, my family have always been good soldiers, but we make lousy spouses."

He sought for the words to reassure her. "You make your own decisions, Lindsey. What your parents or grandparents did doesn't automatically determine what you will do. I don't need an answer now. Think about it — that's all I'm asking."

"I will."

He managed a smile and tried to recapture their easy banter. "Do I still get a kiss when we stop for gas?"

A grin pulled at the corner of her lips. "I'll think about that, too."

Brian settled back in his seat. There were a lot of miles to go and nothing to do but look at the passing winter scenery and think. Her decision was much too important to risk pressing her for an answer. Instead, he said, "Why don't you call your brother and tell him that Dakota is on his way to the parade."

The walkie-talkie crackled on the dash as Karen's voice came over it. "I've already called him. He's as excited as a five-year-old on Christmas morning."

Brian chuckled as Lindsey grabbed the radio and demanded. "Karen, have you been listening this whole time?"

"I heard someone mention stopping for gas and that was all. I just turned this talkie thing on to report that Dakota seems happy as a clam in his snug, padded . . . holder thing."

Lindsey looked as if she wasn't certain she believed her sibling. "All right. I'll trade places with you when we make our first stop."

"How long will that be?"

Brian checked the gas gauge. "About three hours."

"That long?"

"Yes, little miss busybody. Try taking a nap," Lindsey suggested.

"Back here with a smelly horse? I don't think so."

Brian listened to their chatter and drew a deep breath. He had three hours to wait until he could collect his kiss. Three hours alone with the woman he loved. He looked down the long four-lane highway and smiled. He was determined to make the most of every minute God had given him.

For the next few hours, he talked about Emily, about Isabella and about his early years on the ranch.

He listened to Lindsey's stories of her childhood as an army brat and her worries about her brother and about Karen. When they finally stopped, he was rewarded with a kiss that was pleasant but far too brief.

After Lindsey took her turn in the trailer, he received a very different version of their youthful experiences from Karen. It was obvious that Lindsey found the military lifestyle to her liking while Karen didn't. He tolerated some not too gentle grilling by Karen about his intentions and listened to some hopefully useful advice about Lindsey, as well. Every four hours they took a short break to let Dakota stretch his legs and let the women change places.

East of St. Louis, Brian finally gave up the wheel to Lindsey, and just outside of Cin-

cinnati, Karen took over for a few hours while Brian rode with Dakota. It wasn't until they were heading into Wheeling, West Virginia, that the weather began to turn bad. Brian didn't know about the growing storm until they stopped to switch drivers at a roadside rest stop. As Karen walked the horse for a few minutes, Brian took Lindsey aside.

"This could slow us down."

She looked up through the flakes that filled the night sky. "How much farther do we have to go?"

"A little over three hundred miles. Five, maybe six hours."

She tilted her watch to see it better in the vehicle's headlights. "We need to be at the staging area by ten at the latest. That's six and a half hours from now."

"We'll make this Dakota's last exercise stop. We go straight through from here. I'll drive next. Dakota has been as quiet as a lamb so far. I think both you girls can ride in the truck from here on out."

For the next hour, he drove into the swirling whiteness as Lindsey and Karen leaned against each other and tried to sleep. The excitement of the trip had worn off hours ago, and Brian struggled to stay awake. He couldn't stop. He had promised Lindsey that Dakota would reach Washington, D.C., in time. He glanced at the clock on the dash and saw it was nearly five-thirty in the morning. They were falling behind schedule. From the radio forecast bulletins he figured they should be driving out of the worst of it soon. If the weathermen were right for a change.

Forcing himself to concentrate, he peered into the snow. After a few more minutes, he found himself blinking repeatedly. The thick flakes flying into his headlights were mesmerizing. He rubbed his face with one hand. The glare reflecting back from the snow was making it hard to focus. If only he wasn't so tired. He closed his heavy eyes for just a second. . . .

CHAPTER FIFTEEN

The sickening lurch of the truck woke Lindsey from her doze. She sat up abruptly, instinctively throwing her arm across Karen.

"Ouch! What was that for?" Karen said, pushing her sister's arm aside and sitting upright.

"I'm sorry." Brian's voice sounded weary and defeated. "I hit a drift pulling over. We have to stop. The storm is making it too dangerous. I'm not risking your lives in this weather."

He leaned forward and turned on the emergency flashers then leaned back with a deep sigh. Thinking of what he had told her about his wife's death, Lindsey leaned toward him and took his hand between her own. "It's okay. We tried. No one is faulting you."

He looked at Lindsey and reached out to cup her cheek with his free hand. "I wish I could have gotten you there."

"I know you do and I love you for that."

She raised her face and met his kiss with only gladness in her heart.

Karen cleared her throat. "At least you two won't freeze to death. The temperature on your side of the truck is rising fast."

Brian slipped his arm behind Lindsey's shoulders and jerked Karen closer by the sleeve of her jacket. "I'll do my best to keep both of you warm."

Tightly sandwiched between them, Lindsey enjoyed a feeling of rightness. She was disappointed they wouldn't make it to Washington, D.C., but she was so very glad they had taken this trip.

She said, "Don't worry about freezing, Karen. I've had survival training."

"Can you make fire with two sticks?" Brian asked, his amusement clear.

"Doing it with two sticks is hard. I'd rather wait until the sun comes up and use a soda can and a chocolate bar."

"What?" the other two said in unison.

"It can be done. I'll show you someday. For now, I think we could all use a little sleep."

"I know I could," Brian said, leaning his head back.

Lindsey settled herself against his shoulder

and drew Karen into the same position against her. This was where she truly wanted to be, held safe in Brian's arms while the storm outside raged on. This was the one place that was the right place for her. She knew it in her soul.

Thank You, Lord, for bringing this man into my life.

Sometime later, she opened her eyes at the sound of a large truck rumbling past them. She looked at the clock. It was a quarter till seven. Brian sat up and pulled his arm from behind her. Flexing it, he grimaced.

"What was that?" Karen mumbled, sitting up and rubbing her eyes.

Brian turned on the windshield wipers and the white blanket enclosing them was swept aside. The first faint light of dawn tinged the sky to the east of them.

"Hey, it stopped snowing," Karen said in delight.

Brian reached down and started the engine. "Yes, it has, and that was a pair of snowplows." He looked at Lindsey. "What do you think?"

"I think we are closer to Washington, D.C., than to Kansas. Let's finish the trip."

He leaned forward. "Karen?"

"Finish what we started. Maybe we'll get

to see the tail end of the parade."

"All right. I'm going to check on Dakota and then we'll get back on the road."

He stepped out of the truck and used his cane to find firm footing. When he closed the door, Karen jerked on Lindsey's arm. "Well, what is your answer going to be?"

"I said let's go to D.C."

"Not that. Your answer to his marriage proposal."

"You were listening in!"

"I promise you I wasn't listening on purpose. I was trying to find a way to turn the silly thing off."

"Right. Like the dial on the side that says Off is so very hard to find."

"It was dark in the trailer, but never mind that. What's your answer?"

"You'll be the second — no, the fourth — person I'll tell after I make my decision."

"Fourth? I'm your only sister."

"You're a pain in the neck."

Karen sat back with a huff. "I think you should say yes."

"I'll take that under advisement."

Karen opened her mouth to say something else, but by that time Brian had returned. Thankfully, she kept what she wanted to say to herself.

Once they were back on the road, their

spirits revived. Within an hour they had driven out of the snow-covered area and onto dry roads. Brian pushed the speed limit trying to make up some of their lost time.

It was eleven o'clock when they reached downtown D.C. and passed through the first of the security stops. It was then they got their first bit of good news.

The marine handing back their papers said, "The start of the parade has been delayed. It's set to go for one o'clock."

"Do you know why?" Brian asked as he took the forms.

"No, sir."

Rolling up his window, Brian said, "Lindsey, call your Captain and tell him we're almost there."

"They aren't going to wait for us."

"Just call them and let them know we're close."

She dialed the number with hands that shook. "Lord, please don't let him have turned off his cell phone yet."

He answered on the third ring. "It's about time you called, Sergeant."

"Sorry, sir. I knew you would be busy."

"Where are you?"

"We just passed the first checkpoint."

"Okay. All I can say is hurry. We aren't

going to be able to wait if we get the order to go."

"I understand, sir."

At the next checkpoint, they waited as a police officer with a bomb-sniffing dog made a circuit through the trailer. Dakota lowered his head to check out the four-legged visitor, but the German shepherd gave him only a cursory glance before moving on.

Karen shifted from one foot to the other as she stood beside Lindsey. "Why won't they hurry up?"

"They are doing their job."

"They could do it a little faster."

Lindsey turned from watching the search to face her sister. She put both hands on Karen's shoulders. "It doesn't matter if we don't make it. Danny will still get a chance to see Dakota after the parade and he'll get to meet Brian. That's reward enough for me."

"Oh, you're just happy because you're in love. Are you guys done yet?" She called over Lindsey's shoulder. "The President is waiting on us."

"Karen!"

"He might be," she said defensively. "You don't know why the start was delayed."

"You're all clear," the officer said.

"Thank you," Karen called sweetly, then hurried to climb in the cab.

Fifteen minutes later they pulled into the staging area and located Lindsey's unit. They were all mounted except for the Captain. A drill team from a high school in Iowa was just stepping out, while their marching band was hurrying to form up behind them. The Commanding General's Mounted Color Guard was next in line. Shane and Avery dismounted and hurried toward the trailer.

Captain Watson motioned for them to hurry and then turned to speak to a parade official. Brian had already opened the door and was backing Dakota out of the trailer. He handed the horse's lead rope to Shane. Avery grabbed the tack and began to saddle the big bay.

Brian moved to speak with Captain Watson then accompanied him back to Lindsey. She stood gazing at Dakota with tears of joy in her eyes. "Wait until Danny sees you. You behave yourself out there and make him proud."

"Sergeant Mandel, you're out of uniform." Captain Watson stood scowling at her.

She looked down at her rumpled dress uniform in confusion.

"You heard me, change into the unit's

performance gear ASAP."

"But I'm not riding."

"Oh, yes you are." Brian pushed her toward the trailer. "Is your uniform in your suitcase?"

"I've got it," Karen cried as she hefted it into the back of the trailer. "Come on, I'll help you."

Captain Watson grinned. "Sergeant, you didn't think you came all this way just to stand on the sidelines, did you?"

"Sort of."

"No. Get dressed. That's an order, soldier."

Brian watched as a Lindsey snapped to attention. She saluted smartly and climbed into the trailer with her sister.

A few minutes later she emerged in period uniform as she pulled on a pair of white gloves. She walked up to Captain Watson.

"Sergeant Mandel reporting as ordered."

"Give the order to mount up, Sergeant."

"Sir, yes, sir."

She barked out the command, mounted Dakota and rode out into the street. At the order to unfurl the colors, three flags were taken from their covers. Captain Watson took the American flag and handed it to Brian. "As a way to say thank-you for all you have done for this unit, would you please present this flag to First Sergeant Mandel."

"It would be my honor, sir."

Brian looked to where Lindsey sat and read the fear in her eyes.

Lindsey called on every ounce of inner strength that she possessed when Brian handed her the symbol of her country — the country her brother and so many other brave young men and women had given so much to defend.

She closed her hand around the staff, but her grip failed and the wind pulled it from her grasp. Brian caught it before it hit the ground.

"I can't do it." Tears sprang up in her eyes, blurring her vision.

"You can do it, honey. God didn't bring you and Dakota this far to fail you now. Have faith, Lindsey. I have faith in you. Give me your hand."

He placed the end of the rod into the metal cup on her stirrup and folded her fingers around the staff. "Which color in our flag stands for courage?"

"The colors have no official meaning, but to me, all of them stand for courage."

"Show me that courage now."

She closed her eyes and willed her grip to strengthen. An instant later, she heard the sound of tearing cloth and looked down. With the flag braced against his shoulder, Brian ripped a piece of tape from a wide, white roll and made a quick loop around her wrist.

"Open your fingers."

She did and he made two quick passes around the staff and then back around her wrist. The tape blended with her white gloves. When she closed her fingers, it didn't show on the pole.

"Now you don't have to be afraid. You couldn't drop it if you tried."

"Brian, you're a genius."

"Be sure and tell Jennifer that when we get back."

"I haven't turned in my reenlistment papers," she said quickly.

"Why not? I hope it wasn't because of anything I said."

"I love the service, but maybe it's time for *me* to make a change in my life."

"Whatever you decide to do, I'm behind you 100 percent. If you want to remain in the army, we'll find a way to make it work for both of us."

"What about your research? You love your work."

"I do, but I love you more. If we are meant

to be together, the Lord will show us the path."

"Proverbs 16:9, A man's heart plans his way, But the LORD directs his steps."

Grinning, he patted Dakota's neck. "He certainly directed my steps to you."

Looking into his love-filled eyes, Lindsey smiled. "Yes, he did. And the answer to your question is yes."

"Yes, what?"

"Yes, I'll marry you."

"You will? But I can't kiss you up on that horse. Lean down here."

"Meet me after the parade," she suggested with a wink. "I love you, Brian Cutter."

"I love you, too. Now, go make me proud."

Nodding, she touched her spurs to Dakota's sides and rode to the head of the column.

"This is for you, Danny," Lindsey whispered.

Suddenly she knew she wasn't alone. The wind died away to a gentle breeze and a deep warmth surrounded her. An inner strength filled her and her grip on the flag's staff tightened. This had all been a part of His plan.

Thank You, Lord, for giving me this day.

Captain Watson gave the command to move out. The Commanding General's

Mounted Color Guard left the staging area and rode out to take their place on Pennsylvania Avenue.

As Brian watched her ride away, his heart was filled with more happiness than he had ever expected to know again. A second later, Karen was pulling at his sleeve.

"Come on. If we hurry, we can find Dad and Danny before Lindsey passes by. They're going to be in front of the Hoover Building. It's only a couple of blocks."

Following her, he tried to hurry, but she soon disappeared into the crowd. Looking up at the tall, imposing structures lining the street, he wondered if he would recognize the Hoover Building when he saw it.

Just when he had decided to rest and watch the presidential detail passing by, Karen appeared at his side. "They're right over here. Come on."

"Right over here" turned out to be another block. He was gritting his teeth against the pain in his hip by the time Karen announced, "There they are."

He slowed down to catch his breath. Karen hurried toward a man in a wheelchair stationed at the curbside and threw her arms around him. When the man didn't hug her in return, Brian realized what a high price Danny Mandel had paid for the idea of freedom in a country half the world away. Karen knelt beside him and motioned to Brian.

Stepping closer, Brian nodded to the man about his own age held strapped upright in a specially designed chair. Karen quickly made the introductions to Danny, his wife and to Lindsey's father.

Danny grinned. "So you're the rabbit guy Lindsey is always talking about."

"I've been called worse."

Abigail extended her hand. "Dr. Cutter, I want to thank you for the information you sent about hippotherapy. We found out that the Old Guard has a program here. We're looking into it."

"That's great." Brian shook her hand then turned to the senior Mandel. Lindsey's father was an imposing man. Brian could only hope he wouldn't object to a civilian marrying his daughter. With his gray hair still short in a military buzz, he looked quite capable of holding his own in any kind of a fight.

"Thanks for getting my daughter and my boy's horse here. It means a lot to us."

"I'm glad I could help."

"Oh, look, here they come." Karen pushed Danny's chair closer to the curb. Marching in a straight line, Lindsey's unit passed by, pride evident in everyone's ramrod-straight bearing. Lindsey was looking straight ahead, but Dakota swung his head toward them and whinnied loudly.

Karen dropped to her brother's side. "He remembers you."

"He did, didn't he? But he never broke stride. He's a trouper. I'm glad he made it into Lindsey's unit. I'm so proud of both of them."

"Not half as proud as Lindsey is of you," Brian said, laying a hand on Danny's shoulder.

On the other side of them, a young man with a press badge stepped closer. "Excuse me, do you have family in the parade?"

Karen rose, smiling at the young man. "My sister."

"Would you mind if I asked you a few questions about her? The magazine I work for is looking for a common-man angle to the Inauguration."

"There's nothing common about my family," Mr. Mandel declared, turning back to the parade.

Karen wrinkled her nose and stepped closer to the reporter. "Don't mind my dad. But he is right. This is no common family. My sister is a sergeant in the army, my brother here, Danny, was also in the army until he was wounded in action. After that, he selflessly donated his beloved horse to my sister's unit at Fort Riley. Then what happened? The horse fell and broke his leg."

She paused to catch her breath. The reporter was quickly making notes.

She looked at Brian and winked. "That's when Dr. Brian *Cutter,* that's Cutter with a *C,* came to our rescue. He used a new gene therapy to heal Dakota's leg in record time."

Looking around at her family, a mischievous glint brightened her eyes. "Did I mention to everyone that he's going to marry Lindsey?"

Hours later, when the parade was finished and the crowds had dispersed, Brian waited beside the equine ambulance while Lindsey visited with her family. Still dressed in her turn-of-the-century uniform, the woman Brian loved with his whole heart finally made her way to his side. He slipped his arm across her shoulders as she slid her arm around his waist and leaned against him. Standing together, they drew comfort and happiness from each other. He looked down at her but she was watching Danny and Dakota.

It was obvious that Danny was tired but just as obvious that he wasn't ready to go home. Joy radiated from his expression. Dakota stood beside his wheelchair nuzzling his former master's face and searching his pockets in hopes of hidden treats. The smile that Abigail flashed at Brian made every minute of the long trip worthwhile.

"Thank you," Lindsey whispered.

"It was nothing," he answered softly.

"Oh, it was certainly something, Dr. Brian Cutter. How can I ever repay you?"

He looked down at her and smiled. "I'm sure I can think of something, darling."

Her soft laughter in response was all he needed to make this day and every day of his life — complete.

Dear Reader,

I hope you enjoyed Lindsey and Brian's journey toward love. The story of *The Color of Courage* was inspired by an actual event. I first met members of a mounted color guard when a detachment led the parade that opened the county fair near my hometown in Abilene, Kansas, in 2005. I assumed the young men dressed in 1860s period cavalry uniforms were local reenactors. I soon learned that they were active duty soldiers from Fort Irwin, California. The men, some recently returned from Iraq, were proud to share information about their unit and others like it. From them I learned about the Commanding General's Mounted Color Guard at Fort Riley, Kansas.

I knew I wanted to do a story about such a unit, but I wasn't sure where to start so I turned to the Internet for some research. It was online that I first read about a horse named Ike from the CGMCG who suffered a fractured pastern and how the Kansas State College of Veterinary Medicine teamed up with the army to save his life. Ike was still in recovery when the rest of his unit went to Washington, D.C., for the 2005 Inaugural parade. When I read that bit of information, my story was born.

I had the privilege of visiting with the men and women of the Commanding General's Mounted Color Guard and I witnessed firsthand their feats of horsemanship. While their skill is truly extraordinary, it is their pride in serving their country and preserving a part of our history that impressed me the most. My words cannot do justice to their sacrifices and dedication.

Innumerable people helped with the research that went into writing this story. I'd like to thank Patrice Scott, Media Relations at K-State, Dr. James Lillich, DVM, MS Associate Professor, Equine Ortho & General Surgery at K-State, the Dept. of Public Relations at Fort Riley, Former unit commander, Shane Pruente, and the men and women currently serving at Fort Riley. Any mistakes I made in writing this book are entirely my own fault.

Blessing to you all,
Patricia Davids

QUESTIONS FOR DISCUSSION

1. Brian had never been able to move past his guilt over his wife's death. Why do you believe he couldn't?

2. Should women in the army be allowed to serve in combat units? Why or why not?

3. Lindsey kept Dakota's condition from her brother until the very last minute. Was she right to do so? Why?

4. Hippotherapy is gaining recognition as a valuable form of rehabilitation. Is there a program in your area? How can you find out?

5. What two characters were most instrumental in getting Lindsey and Brian together?

6. Brian found it hard to believe that faith

in God and military service go hand in hand. Do you believe that they do? Why or why not?

7. What lesson did Lindsey have to learn before she was ready to fall in love? How was that expressed in the story?

8. How did the humor in the story add to its enjoyment?

9. Did any element in the story affect how you view military service? Why?

10. Was Lindsey's decision to leave the army the right one? Why or why not?

ABOUT THE AUTHOR

Patricia Davids continues to work as a part-time nurse in the NICU, while writing full-time. She enjoys researching new stories, traveling to new locations and meeting fans along the way. She and her husband of thirty-two years live in Wichita, Kansas, along with the newest addition to the household, a stray cat named Spooky. Pat always enjoys hearing from her readers. You can contact her by mail at P.O. Box 16714 Wichita, Kansas 67216, or visit her on the Web at www.patriciadavids.com.